A Winter's Miracle

A Nantucket Sunset Series

Katie Winters

ALL RIGHTS RESERVED. No part of this publication may be reproduced, distributed, or transmitted in any form or by any means, including photocopying, recording, or other electronic or mechanical methods, without the prior written permission of the publisher.

Copyright © 2024 by Katie Winters

This is a work of fiction. Any resemblance of characters to actual persons, living or dead is purely coincidental. Katie Winters holds exclusive rights to this work. Unauthorized duplication is prohibited.

Chapter One

It was the week before Christmas, and glistening snow blanketed the island of Nantucket. Anna could feel expectation for the holiday in every corner of the island—in the warm conversation at the coffee shop, the bustle of the historic downtown, and every nook and cranny of the decorated Copperfield House. After all, the Copperfield family had spent an entire weekend together, selecting the perfect Christmas tree, stringing lights, and taking plenty of breaks to eat Christmas cookies (baked by Grandma Greta, of course). But Christmas felt distant this year—like something Anna couldn't fully bring into her heart. At eight months pregnant, she was exhausted, her ankles were swelled, and her consciousness stunted with fear. In just one month, she would give birth to a baby boy. And because her fiancé had suddenly passed away last April, she would have to learn to parent alone.

In her bedroom at The Copperfield House, Anna sat on the edge of her bed, listening to the chaos through the halls and bedrooms of the immense home. It sounded like

James was late for high school. It was his last day before classes let out for the holidays, and he yelled back to his mother, telling her it was all right, that he'd done all his homework, and that nobody cared if he was late on the last day.

Quentin's booming voice came next, "We told you to get up an hour ago!" Anna smiled inwardly. At twenty-four, with so much "real life" behind her, high school now seemed like a romantic time of her life. An era of not knowing and of hope.

Just then, her grandmother, Greta, hollered downstairs, telling anyone who cared to listen, "There's more coffee!" It was eight, meaning Greta would disappear into her office to write away the rest of the morning. She always woke up early to make sure the rest of the family was cared for.

Anna pulled her hair into a ponytail and waddled downstairs to pour herself a cup of tea and a large glass of water. There, Aunt Ella and Uncle Will sat at the kitchen table with the newspaper sections strewn in front of them. They'd just returned from several months of touring with their band. They were happy and easy to talk to, swapping stories about their trips to Memphis, Chicago, and New Orleans and asking Anna about her past few months in Nantucket.

"I've been busy," Anna said with a laugh, referring to her giant stomach.

Aunt Ella chuckled and turned the page of her newspaper. "Your mom said you've been hard at work. Lots of writing?"

Anna raised her shoulders. Her dreams of becoming a travel writer had sort of diminished in the wake of Dean's death. The accident happened on Orcas Island, where

A Winter's Miracle

Anna was assigned to her first big-time writing gig. She couldn't help but blame herself. Maybe if she hadn't wanted to be a travel writer so badly. Maybe if she hadn't forced her and Dean's relationship to move so quickly. Maybe then, Dean would still be alive.

But it had felt like a wild rush of romanticism. They'd met a year and a half ago in Seattle and abandoned the rest of the world, their friends, and their responsibilities, falling in love in the only way two twentysomethings could. When Dean had asked her to marry him on Orcas Island, she'd felt her life stretching out before her like the stars in the black sky. And then, he'd died.

She hadn't known she was pregnant. She hadn't known she was about to enter the single most challenging era of her life. There had been nothing to do but keep going.

"I hope you don't mind that your mom invited me to the Christmas market later," Aunt Ella said. "She said you're writing something about it?"

"It's for *Nantucket Insider Magazine*," Anna said, clutching her mug of tea. "They want a write-up of the Christmas market. Something simple. Easy."

"Looking forward to it," Aunt Ella said.

Anna disappeared in her bedroom to go over the edits for her most recent travel article, which was to be published in *Travel + Leisure* magazine. The topic was springtime travel in Nantucket. Anna had written separate guides for families, parents of young children, parents of teenagers, newlyweds, and singles. She'd wept during the newlywed's section, imagining herself and Dean exploring Nantucket and Martha's Vineyard together, eating seafood, and hiking the white sand beaches. It seemed tremendously unfair that she wouldn't be allowed that life.

Until recently, Anna had had a therapist to review this with. They'd discussed Anna's inner rage for her circumstances and tried to build fresh hope for Anna's new reality. But Anna's therapist had moved to Los Angeles for her husband's job—and Anna hadn't gone through the trouble to make a new connection. She'd decided to call herself "healed."

Anna's cell phone pinged with a text. To her surprise, it was Violet Carpenter, Dean's mother.

> VIOLET: Hi, honey! How are you feeling?

Anna's heartbeat quickened. Anna hadn't seen Violet since Dean's funeral back in April, a time that now seemed gray and amorphous. It was often difficult for her to remember it, as though grief had robbed her of short-term memory. Dean's parents, Violet and Larry Carpenter, lived in Dayton, Ohio, where Dean was raised. Because Anna and Dean hadn't even been together a year at the time of their engagement, Anna didn't know them well. She hadn't even gone to the wake, choosing instead to go on a mad road trip across the continent to return home.

Violet and Larry had seemed ecstatic about the pregnancy (as happy as two people who'd lost their son could be, that is). Violet had even made plans to come to Nantucket to visit. But with Anna's travel writing, Violet's grief, and the sheer fact that they were essentially strangers, they still hadn't made it work.

> ANNA: I'm doing well, thanks. Just one more month till the baby.

> VIOLET: I'm over the moon.

> VIOLET: Listen, honey. I've been such a mess over here. But you and the baby have never been far from my mind.

> VIOLET: What do you think about me visiting a few days after Christmas? I'd love to shower you with baby presents and love.

Anna raised both of her eyebrows in surprise. Violet's face flashed through her mind's eye. She was around Anna's mother's age, forty-six, with dark-blond hair and eyes the color of a pine forest. Dean had looked more like his father than his mother, but he'd often told Anna that his personality was more like his mother's. They both loved a little too hard, he'd said.

> ANNA: The Copperfield House is enormous. We would love to host you.

It never occurred to Anna that once she invited Violet into The Copperfield House, she would have a hard time getting her to leave. Perhaps it should have. After all, The Copperfield House was an escape from the sinister realities that lurked outside of Nantucket. It was that way for everyone.

* * *

The Christmas market was located in the Historic District. It featured nearly thirty stalls where bundled-up and smiling vendors sold mulled wine, hot cocoa, pastries, chocolates, arts and crafts, and gifts. Anna suspected it was an intense time for them. They needed to make as much money as they could during the Christmas season. But Anna's travel article couldn't go into the economics of Christmas festivals. She needed to uphold the spirit and beauty of the Christmas festival. She needed to promote tourism on Nantucket—even though Nantucket definitely didn't struggle in that regard.

Anna, Grandma Greta, Aunt Alana, Aunt Ella, and Anna's mother, Julia, wandered through the Christmas market that afternoon, pausing to inspect hand-knitted mittens, Christmas decorations, and little Christmas treats. It wasn't long before Greta discovered that one of the stalls was owned by a French woman selling traditional French Christmas decorations. Greta was quick to tell the woman that she'd once lived in France and remained fluent in the language. The woman responded in French, and the two of them spoke happily. Greta's smile lit up the gray sky above.

"Here." Julia appeared before Anna and handed her a mug of hot cocoa filled with marshmallows. "Are you getting cold?"

"Oh! Thanks." Anna laughed and adjusted the cup in her hands. "Not too bad, yet."

Worry flickered through Julia's eyes. After Dean's death, Julia had become Anna's protector and sort of "life partner." They'd certainly become better friends than they'd ever been back in the suburbs of Chicago, where Julia had raised Anna and her brother and sister. That was before the divorce and Julia's brave move back to Nantucket. Anna had been just a typical teenager, picking fights with her mother and father while dreaming of a different life.

It wasn't that she blamed herself for being a usual teenager. You couldn't change the past, anyway.

"Are you getting inspired?" Aunt Ella asked playfully, smiling over her own cup of cocoa.

"I think we'd better ply her with more chocolate and treats first," Aunt Alana said. "That'll really help her with the article."

"I won't turn them down," Anna said with a wry laugh.

Ella's eyes danced as she took in the marvelous scene. "I hope Laura and Danny will come back here with me when they get home," she said, referring to her son and daughter, both of whom were away at university in Manhattan. "Gosh, I've missed them. Laura said we call them too much from tour." She rolled her eyes into a smile.

"I've been counting down the days till Henry and Rachel get here," Julia said. "The Copperfield House will be bustling. I hope Mom will let us help her cook this year."

Greta returned from her conversation with the French woman, brimming with joy. "Fat chance," she said with a laugh. "Maybe I'll let you slice a few cloves of garlic. But only if you do it my way."

"What a control freak," Aunt Alana teased, nudging her mother with her elbow.

Anna snapped her fingers. "That reminds me." Her two aunts, mother, and grandmother regarded her curiously. "Dean's mother texted me today." Anna hated how her voice wavered when she said his name. She didn't want anyone's pity.

"Oh! What did Violet say?" Julia asked. She'd never met Dean's parents, but Anna had told her everything she knew about them—which wasn't much beyond their names and occupations.

"She said she wants to come to Nantucket," Anna said.

"I can't believe it's taken her so long to visit," Greta said, folding her arms over her chest. "Her first grandchild will be here any minute."

Anna waved her hand. She didn't want anyone to speak ill of Violet. The woman had lost her son.

"Is she going to stay till the baby comes?" Aunt Ella asked.

"She said 'a few days,'" Anna offered, flapping two of her fingers for air quotes.

"She should stay," Julia said, sounding breathless. "She'll want to know her grandson. She'll want to be here when it happens."

The five Copperfield women were quiet for a moment, considering the weight of the new baby. With Dean gone and Anna giving birth to his baby in his absence, it was impossible to know how to feel. Joy was essential, as was grief.

They continued to wander through the stalls. Anna made several notes about the market in her phone app, feeling the article come to life in her mind. As she paused to type out another note about the chocolate delicacies, she heard a woman speaking in low tones to a little boy, telling him to be patient and to wait his turn. "It's okay, baby," the young mother said, the sweep of her hair coming over her face. The little boy, with adorable, plump cheeks, couldn't have been more than three or four. Anna's heart melted as she watched them. She imagined herself three or four years from now, guiding her son through the market stalls, helping him understand the magic of Christmas. She envisioned telling him about his father for the first time.

Oh, but what would she tell her son about Dean? Already, she felt as though she'd lost so much of him. Sometimes, she couldn't even hear his voice in her head. She never told anyone this. It felt shameful.

Julia's pocket jangled with a phone call as Julia, Aunt Ella, and Aunt Alana approached with a round of mulled wine. Julia grumbled and asked Anna to hold her wine. "Just for a second." She then retrieved her phone and blew all the air from her lungs.

"Who is it?" Anna asked.

"That client I was telling you about," Julia said. "I have to take it."

Anna shifted her weight nervously, trying to remember which client her mother had mentioned. Julia ran her own publishing house, which had nearly failed but risen from the ashes after Grandpa Bernard had published his bestselling novel last year. Since then, Julia had been up to her ears in book sales and successful clients. Everyone wanted to work with the great Julia Copperfield.

"Hey, Smith," Julia began, sounding reticent. It was as though she wanted to prepare her heart for bad news.

Anna listened to Julia's half of the conversation, gleaning that Smith wasn't as far into the book as they'd planned.

"The thing is, Smith," Julia said, rubbing her temple, "if we're going to publish by next Christmas, we really need to hit these metrics. I know you know that."

Anna's heart thudded at her mother's businesslike tone. She was guilty of missing a deadline or two, and she remembered the adrenaline and the guilt of it. She remembered feeling she wasn't good enough to succeed.

"All right. If you promise," Julia finished, rolling her eyes toward her sisters. "Take care."

Julia shoved her phone back in her pocket and took her mulled wine back from Anna. Her cheeks were pale.

"That didn't sound good," Greta said, returning to the fold from another craft stall, where she'd purchased a handmade scarf.

"I have this new client," Julia explained. "Smith Watson."

"Great name," Aunt Ella said.

"It's a sellable name," Greta agreed.

"I signed him a few months ago," Julia went on. "He shows tremendous promise. But he's been through a lot in life. I don't know if he can pull everything together for me. For himself. For his career." She scrunched up her face.

"He's writing a novel?" Greta asked.

"A memoir," Julia said. "He draws from his incredibly difficult past in a way I find incendiary."

"What happened to him?" Aunt Alana asked. A wrinkle formed between her eyebrows.

Julia waved her hand. "I can't even get into it. Suffice it to say, it's a miracle he's still alive today."

Greta looked contemplative. She glanced at Anna, who furrowed her brow, trying to read her grandmother's expression. It always seemed like Greta was up to something. Like she was ten steps ahead of everyone else.

"Why don't you invite him to The Copperfield House?" Greta suggested.

Julia raised both eyebrows.

"We only have two people staying in the residency

right now," Greta pointed out, "so there's plenty of space for him to stay. And maybe here, you can help keep him focused on his memoir. You can guide him gently toward his goals." Greta beamed.

"Mom! That's a brilliant idea," Julia said.

"If he's as talented as you say he is, he belongs at The Copperfield House," Greta said, touching Anna's shoulder.

"What about his family?" Aunt Alana asked. "Are they around?"

"There's not much family to speak of," Julia offered. "Just his mother. And she's the poisonous center of the memoir."

"I take it they don't talk," Aunt Ella said.

"Not at all," Julia said. "Smith says he won't go within an hour of her place."

Something cold and hard dropped into Anna's stomach. Protectively, she touched her pregnant belly and closed her eyes. She hated thinking about a future in which her son hated her, in which he told people he wouldn't go within an hour of her place. What if she failed as a mother? What if she had no idea what she was doing? What if she unknowingly made him run away?

Chapter Two

Back in Julia's office at The Copperfield House, she pulled up the chapters Smith Watson had sent her thus far and rubbed her palms together. Already, she could envision the book's cover, with its working title, *Mediocre*. She was thinking bright, bold colors. She was thinking New York Times Best Seller list.

But in order to sell, Julia needed Smith to write at least sixty thousand words—and he'd only finished fifteen. They had a soft deadline in April, just a few days before her wedding, and a harder deadline by May, at which time the editor needed to take over. The book was planned to go to print by August, with initial sales in October, just in time for the holiday season. *Mediocre* was set to bring in the biggest sales of Julia's career. She couldn't wait.

The title *Mediocre* had been taken from Smith's mother's own lips. Apparently, that was the refrain his mother had given him, regardless of what he'd done or how hard he'd worked. He was never good enough. He never pleased her. And that manifested in about a thousand horrific ways throughout Smith's young life.

Smith was twenty-six and living in Brooklyn with three roommates and a spunky dog named Luka. Julia had seen Luka on video chat several times, watching Luka shower Smith with kisses. Smith had said, "He's the only thing in the world who loves me." Julia's heart had felt bruised.

Now, Julia pulled up Smith's phone number and called him back. She regretted that she'd spoken to him so sternly before. She needed to nurture him in ways his mother hadn't.

Smith answered on the third ring. "Hello?" In the background, Julia heard numerous barks, presumably all from Luka. "Sorry, I'm at the dog park."

"Smith, hey!" Julia hated how optimistic she sounded. "Listen. I'm sorry about earlier."

Smith's tone melted. "It's all right. I get it. You gave me an enormous opportunity, and I'm messing it up."

"You're not!" Julia assured him. "Really." She chewed her lower lip. "Have I ever told you about where I live?"

"Uh? No."

Julia told him as much as she could. She told him about Bernard and Greta's idea to form half of their home into an artist residency, where they welcomed artists, writers, musicians, and filmmakers from around the world. There, they communed, swapped ideas, and created. Julia wanted Smith to come work on his memoir there. That way, he wouldn't get distracted.

"I don't know," Smith said, sounding depleted. "I don't have money for an artist residency."

"We wouldn't charge you," Julia explained. "And you can leave any time you want."

Smith paused for a moment. The barking subsided, and Julia imagined him roaming the frigid streets of Brooklyn, guiding Luka back home.

"Can I bring my dog?" he asked.

"The more, the merrier."

* * *

Julia's secretary back in Chicago arranged everything for Smith's trip. She bought bus and ferry tickets, sent documents to Smith's email, and pinged him with several reminder messages to ensure he left on time. Julia thanked her endlessly, reminding her, "This publishing house would have failed a long time ago without you!"

To Julia's surprise, Smith had requested traveling to The Copperfield House on Christmas Day "to avoid crowded buses." He was worried Luka would freak out with too many people around. Having never owned a dog herself, Julia had to take his word for it.

Smith was set to arrive at eight o'clock on Christmas evening. Julia watched the skies with rapt attention throughout the day. Violent-looking gray and black clouds simmered overhead, spitting so much snow on the island that the announcer on Greta's kitchen radio warned the ferries might close down. Julia winced.

"I don't know what we'll do if Smith can't make it," she said.

"It'll work out," Greta assured her, smearing a rag over the kitchen counter and giving Julia a soft smile.

In the living room, the entire Copperfield clan was gathered around the Christmas tree as a fire blared in the fireplace, crackling and popping against the stones.

Bernard was at the baby grand piano, playing "Have Yourself a Merry Little Christmas" quietly as the family sipped wine, exchanged stories, or read quietly. Julia's heart filled at the sight of so many people she loved in one place.

Her son, Henry, appeared at the bottom of the staircase, smiling abashedly. He'd been on the phone with his father, Jackson, who was back in Beijing, working as a traveling newscaster. It surprised everyone that Julia and Jackson were on good terms these days. Jackson even sent her a "congratulations" card after she and Charlie had officially gotten engaged.

Julia thought she should have always been with Charlie. But Jackson had given her children. They'd built and shared an entire life together for decades. She would never forget it.

Charlie was seated at the far end of the couch next to his two daughters, both of whom Julia had gotten to know well since she and Charlie had rekindled their relationship a year and a half ago. It bruised her heart to think about their mother, who'd died. Julia would never fill the hole she'd left behind.

"Have you heard from Smith?" Charlie caught her eye.

"I'm worried," Julia admitted, palming the back of her neck. "The snow's picking up, and he isn't responding to my texts."

Anna sat on the plush green chair near the window. Her emerald gown highlighted her baby bump beautifully, and her hair cascaded down her shoulders and back. The look on her face was just the same as it always was—dreamy, edged with sorrow. Julia still couldn't believe that

Anna had gone through so much by the age of twenty-four. She'd made up her mind to protect her. But Julia knew what Anna really needed was love. And Dean had passed away, taking her love with him.

For Christmas, everyone had given Anna even more baby gifts. Julia knew that was what Anna wanted. She wanted preparation for the next few months of her life. But Julia couldn't help but remember the little girl she'd raised, who'd been given books and dolls and colored pencils. She'd once been allowed to dream only for herself.

"Let's go down and pick him up," Charlie said.

"I don't want to interrupt your Christmas," Julia offered. "I don't mind going alone."

"You aren't going by yourself. Not on Christmas," Charlie said. "The girls want to head home anyway. Don't they?"

Charlie, Julia, and Charlie's girls bundled up for the snowy evening and piled into Charlie's truck. The radio played "Jingle Bells," but a sadder, slower version than the childish, jangly version. It tugged at Julia's heartstrings.

After they dropped Charlie's daughters off at the home where he and his wife had raised them, Charlie drove slowly through the snowstorm toward the harbor. Julia clenched her fists, her eyes on the inky water as they approached. A single ferry grew closer and closer, becoming a large, glowing object on the black water.

"I can't wait to meet your latest genius," Charlie teased as he cut the engine.

Julia chuckled into her hands. "You think I'm crazy, putting all my hope into a twenty-six-year-old memoirist?"

Charlie placed his hand around Julia's head and

gazed into her eyes. "I've never thought you were crazy," he said.

"Hold your judgment till after he gets here." Julia chuckled.

The ferry drifted against the edge of the dock, and the ramp came off the side like a long tongue. Julia and Charlie waited, focusing on the ramp as the few people insane enough to travel on a snowy Christmas night burst from the edge. Most of them were hidden beneath hats or hoods. But suddenly, a golden retriever raced from the side of the boat and scampered into a snow drift, drawing some of the snow onto his nose and shaking his tail.

"That must be Luka!" Julia cried, putting her weight into the door and hopping out.

As Julia and Charlie raced through the snow, a young man of about six feet stomped down the ramp, going after the dog. "I told you!" he cried to someone Julia couldn't see. "He doesn't need to be on a leash. I trained him."

Julia would have recognized Smith's voice anywhere after their endless conversations via video chat about the state of his memoir. But unlike when they'd spoken, Smith sounded volatile and angry now, as though he'd spent the better part of the journey arguing with someone on board.

Charlie gave her a look, and Julia winced.

"He's probably had a hard trip," she muttered.

Smith hurried toward Luka and swept his hands through his fur, mumbling to him. Julia couldn't hear what he said. As she got closer, something about his face gave her pause. It was the face of a much older man, etched with wrinkles, as though Smith had gone through tremendous pain that had left his twenty-six-year-old face haggard. Based on what Julia knew about him, this stood to reason. But it was strange to see it in person. It made it more real.

"Smith?" Julia finally said his name, and Smith turned from his dog and blinked through the snow at her. He didn't smile. "It's me. It's Julia. Hi. Welcome to Nantucket."

Smith strode toward Charlie and Julia, and Luka matched his pace, wagging his tail.

"Merry Christmas," Charlie tried.

Smith stopped short in front of them. Snow piled up on his black hair, and his blue eyes were especially soulful and strange in the lanterns of the harbor.

"Hey," Smith said finally.

"Did something happen on the boat?" Julia asked tentatively.

Smith rolled his shoulders back. "It doesn't matter." He looked defeated.

"Let's get back home, shall we?" Julia suggested, forcing a smile. "My mother made an enormous feast with enough leftovers to feed us for days."

Smith stiffened and glanced from Charlie to Julia and back again. "I don't have to hang out with anyone. Do I?"

"No," Julia blurted, her heart rate quickening. "Nobody expects anything from you. For you, The Copperfield House is, first and foremost, a residency. You can come and go as you please, write in your room or in the library, and even use a separate kitchen from the rest of us."

"And we bought Luka dog food," Charlie remembered. "It's in your kitchen, next to a brand-new dog bowl."

Smith's lips turned into a half smile. Julia could have hugged Charlie right then for knowing just what to say.

"This is my fiancé, by the way," Julia remembered.

"Charlie." Charlie stuck out his hand and shook Smith's. Smith's grip looked formidable. "I hope you're happy here," Charlie said. "You just let us know what you need, and we can make it happen."

Chapter Three

Anna was in the kitchen when her mother and Charlie returned with the newcomer, Smith. She dried a dish, watching out the window as they walked around the house to the artist residency entrance. A dog scampered after them, its eyes shining. It seemed Smith didn't want to socialize. Then again, nothing was worse than meeting twenty-some strangers on Christmas night after traveling all day.

Eloise and Greta returned to the kitchen with piles of used plates and forks from a final round of pumpkin pie. Eloise was Greta's long-lost little sister. After a series of strange events, Eloise picked Anna up in Ohio after Dean's funeral and drove her back to Nantucket. Since then, she and Greta had picked up the pieces of their sisterly relationship and become thick as thieves once again. Sometimes, it felt like they had entire conversations in the air between them without uttering a single word. It was freaky.

"The new writer is here," Greta announced.

"Can't blame him for hiding himself away," Eloise said quietly. "But I think I'll make him a plate."

The door between the artist residency and the family house opened, bringing Charlie and Julia back into the fold. Julia's cheeks were red, but she smiled happily and slapped her thighs.

"He made it," she announced.

"And his little dog, too," Charlie joked, closing the door after them.

"How does he seem?" Greta asked.

"Slightly frustrated," Julia admitted, lowering her voice as she entered the kitchen. "He said on the drive over here that he hasn't left Brooklyn in more than three years. And I think he got into some kind of argument with a ferry worker."

Greta wrinkled her nose but remained quiet. Anna remembered that Greta had hardly left The Copperfield House during the twenty-five years Bernard had been locked away in prison. Maybe she felt a kinship with Smith. Or maybe she just thought he was ungrateful. It was hard to say.

"We don't put up with attitude like that in The Copperfield House," Greta reminded them. "You remember what happened a few months back?"

Anna did. Greta had kicked out a promising young writer who'd made it his mission to mess with the hearts of the two young female writers who lived on his floor. Greta had done it swiftly, righting wrongs in the span of just a few minutes. Anna admired her grandmother for that. She still remembered what Dean said about her when he'd come to Nantucket to meet her family. *"Your grandmother is unlike any person I've ever met in my life."*

One after another, members of the Copperfield family retreated to their bedrooms to sleep. They rubbed their eyes and whispered thanks to Greta, wishing everyone a Merry Christmas as they limped up the staircase. Not wanting to be left behind, Anna joined them, brushing her teeth and locking herself away in her bedroom. But when she sat on the edge of the bed, her baby stirred and kicked, and her thoughts raced. Sleep seemed further than ever.

Still wearing her pajamas, Anna tiptoed downstairs, made a mug of tea, and sat on the enclosed back porch, which was just warm enough for late-night rendezvous. Anna should know. She ended up there about three times a week when her mind got ahead of itself, and her fears simmered.

The heavy snow on the beach glinted with the light from a fresh moon. The clouds had spread out and disintegrated for now, but the air was wet, proof that more would come soon. Already, Anna's phone projected eight more inches tomorrow, and the ferries had already been canceled for the next two days.

Nobody could get off the island, even if they wanted to. And nobody could come to the island either. This made Anna feel as though they were living in a snow globe, separated from the rest of the world.

As Anna gazed into the inky night, a figure appeared in her periphery. Anna sat bolt upright, watching as the figure ambled through the snow. He looked to be about six feet, with scraggly hair. He could have been anyone. But a moment later, a golden retriever shot into view, dancing in the snow drifts and gazing up at his companion.

It was Smith and Luka.

Smith didn't know Anna was just twenty feet away, watching him. The idea of being a spy thrilled her, if only because so much of her life was not so thrilling these days. Anna stood and strolled toward the window, watching as Luka licked snow from Smith's fingers as Smith laughed down upon him. The light in his eyes seemed different from the "attitude" her mother had reported earlier. Clearly, Smith was out of his element, in a strange place, and up against a tremendous task. Anna had never written a book before, let alone a memoir. And she had to think memoir was the more difficult of the two. It demanded that you reveal your soul.

Smith paused on his snowy walk to gaze up at the moon. Anna ached to know what was on his mind and if The Copperfield House was as romantic as Julia had promised him. Although all her cousins and siblings were at The Copperfield House for the holidays, Anna couldn't help but feel incredibly lonely, up against motherhood. And she felt her loneliness echoing across Smith's face.

Julia hadn't told Anna much about Smith's life or his memoir. She'd insinuated that he'd been through a lot, that he'd nearly fallen apart with grief, and that grief was the topic of his new book. What could it be?

Anna was suddenly filled with the desire to go into the snow and introduce herself. She didn't want Smith to feel lonely here. She wanted him to know he had her; he had people. Nobody wanted his misery to continue.

Anna pressed against the porch door and walked into the darkness. The door springs screamed, and Luka barked out across the night. Smith's eyes were upon her, studying her, and Anna felt exposed.

But as Anna stepped down the stairs that led to the

snow-covered sand below, her foot skidded against a patch of ice. All at once, she tumbled, smashing her tailbone against an icy embankment. A scream burst from her throat. That was followed by terror for her baby's health. Why had she been so stupid?

Anna gasped for breath, suddenly petrified. Tears streamed down her cheeks.

Luka bounded through the snow. His fat pink tongue was upon her, lapping up her tears, and her heart rate calmed for a moment, allowing her to close her eyes as she steadied herself. A split second later, Smith's footsteps came through the snow. He knelt beside her and placed his hand on her shoulder.

"Hey. Hey, are you all right?"

Anna told herself to act normal, to breathe. Slowly, she opened her eyes again and peered into his gorgeous blue ones, suddenly overwhelmed. She could smell the chill from the air on his hair and something else—bad coffee from the ferry. She had the sudden instinct to draw her arms around him and burrow her face in his chest.

"I'm sorry," Anna said, although she wasn't sure who she was talking to. Perhaps herself. Perhaps her baby. Perhaps Smith.

Before Smith could say anything else, the porch door screeched open again to reveal Bernard, Anna's grandfather. With a pipe between his lips, he stared down at Anna in surprise. He was on his knees in a flash, helping her to her feet.

"Goodness gracious," Bernard said. "What happened here?"

The light in Smith's eyes dimmed, and he stumbled back and cleaned his knees of snow.

"I was being stupid," Anna explained timidly.

A Winter's Miracle

Bernard and Smith were speechless. They gaped at her. Anna wanted to make a joke, but everything fell flat in her mind.

"Is everything okay?" Smith asked, crossing his arms over his chest. His tone was completely different, as though he didn't want her grandfather to know he cared.

Anna thought that was curious. Why wouldn't Smith want others to perceive his empathy? Did he see it as a sign of weakness? And did that have something to do with the topic of his memoir?

She hated to admit he'd piqued her interest. It had been a long time since she felt curious about the world. Great-aunt Eloise had said her curiosity would come back one of these days—that it would flow like a rushing stream when the time was right. But Anna hadn't imagined her curiosity would return on the snow-filled night of Christmas.

"I'd better be going," Smith said, turning on his heel and guiding his dog to the side entrance of the house.

"Let's get you up," Grandpa Bernard said, taking both of Anna's smaller hands in his massive ones and lifting her. "Does anything hurt?"

Anna shook her head. "Just my ego."

Bernard chuckled and brushed snow from her shoulders and arms. "Welcome to being an adult, honey," he said. "We're all nursing our wounds."

Long after Anna returned to her bedroom, she could hardly breathe, remembering Smith's eyes floating so close to hers. She felt like a fool.

Chapter Four

Julia decided to let Smith settle in over the next few days. She knew pushing any artistic process before it had fully percolated wasn't good. Anyway, she was lost in the throes of Christmas family reunions, eating cookies with Rachel, having deep conversations with Henry on the back porch, and taking care of Anna. Being a mother was always her number-one job—and she would soon become a grandmother. She wanted to relish this time before putting her full effort into work.

It was no surprise to anyone that Smith kept to himself. He was secluded in his room, cooking his own meals in the residency kitchen (mostly spaghetti, it sounded like) and hardly communicating with the other residency artists.

"I don't know why I assumed the magic of this old place would work on him." Julia sighed, leaning against the kitchen counter as Greta made a decadent sauce to go with the potatoes. "I figured he'd step inside and immediately feel, I don't know, the energy you and Dad put into this place over the years. I figured he'd finish his memoir by the end of January." She laughed wryly, realizing she was only half joking.

Greta arched her brow and stirred the sauce. Just that morning, Julia had shown Greta some of the pages of Smith's manuscript, and Greta had remained quiet about them thus far. Julia burned to know what was on Greta's mind. It wasn't often she kept her opinions to herself.

"The kid has been through a lot," Greta finally said, removing her spoon from the pot and tasting the edge. "It must be outrageous for him to see all the Copperfields together. He's never known a big family like that. I mean, he's never felt that kind of warmth."

Julia rolled her shoulders back, remembering the scene Smith had painted of his home back in Pennsylvania. It seemed like something out of a nightmare.

"And you're sure he's okay with publishing all that? About his mother?" Greta asked tentatively.

"He sees it as a way of exorcising his demons," Julia said, quoting Smith precisely. "He's twenty-six going on fifty-five."

Greta wrinkled her nose and gazed out the window, where another late December snowfall filled the edges of the windows.

That afternoon, Julia met with Smith in her office for the first time. He appeared in a ratty red T-shirt and a pair of loose jeans, with Luka hot on his heels and his tongue lolling from his mouth. As Smith sat, he patted Luka's head gingerly and looked at Julia with full eye contact, which startled her. It was rare to meet someone so unafraid.

Julia clicked her pen and glanced back at the manuscript pages she'd printed to go over with Smith that morning. She wanted to discuss the story's arc, where to position the backstory to enhance the emotional effect, and how best they should proceed strategically now that Smith and Julia were under one roof.

"This is such a pleasure for me, Smith," Julia began, stuttering slightly. "It's rare I get to spend so much one-on-one time with one of my writers. And like I've said a million times before, I see real promise here. I could imagine it at the top of every best-seller list, selling at airports and traded between everyone from fifteen-year-olds to eighty-five-year-olds. But we have to get in gear if we're going to make that happen."

Julia put an authoritative slant to her voice, one she'd previously had to use occasionally with Henry when he'd been an unruly teenager. It felt funny to return to this version of herself. She'd thought she'd left this particular Julia in the suburbs of Chicago.

Smith remained quiet, petting his dog as he gazed at Julia baldly. Julia swallowed a lump in her throat.

She tried another tactic.

"How are you liking Nantucket so far?"

Smith blinked. "It's obviously beautiful." He said it as though it were a ready-made fact.

"Yes." Julia stuttered. "I loved growing up here."

That was a lie in many ways. If Julia was honest with Smith, she would tell him about Marcia Conrad framing her father, about how she'd run away at seventeen, and how miserable she'd been when her family had fallen apart.

But Smith came from a family without pieces to put back together again. She didn't want to force him to compare and contrast stories.

"Who is that?" Smith nodded out the window

toward the beach below, where a violent sea wind rushed off the water and crashed against the frame of the old house.

Julia followed his gaze to find Anna walking alongside a woman Julia recognized as Dean's mother. Her heart lifted. Anna had said Violet would arrive today, and Julia was grateful everything had gone according to plan. Even now, Violet paused and placed her hand over her eyes as a shield, gazing out across the waves. She looked captivated.

More than once, Julia had tried to put herself in Violet's shoes—to imagine that she'd lost her child instead. Each time had brought Julia to her knees. It was nothing a parent should ever have to endure.

"That's my daughter, Anna," Julia answered.

Smith nodded.

"As you can see, she'll become a mother any day now. We're all quite excited."

Smith remained wordless, although his eyes flickered. Julia struggled to read him.

"And walking with her is Anna's friend," Julia said, stuttering with the lie.

"A friend?" Smith arched his eyebrow, sensing something wrong. Anna was only twenty-four, after all. What was she doing, being friends with a woman old enough to be her mother?

"She was engaged to her son," Julia explained.

"Past tense," Smith observed.

"Unfortunately, yes. There was a tragedy."

Smith leaned back in his chair and crossed his arms over his chest. A flash of humanity came into his eyes, and he remained rapt, watching Anna and Violet out the window. Violet held her hand over Anna's stomach, and her eyes shone. This was the grandson she'd never thought she'd be allowed to have. It was a blessing.

"Your daughter is a writer?" Smith asked.

"Yes." Julia was surprised Smith knew anything about Anna. "She writes travel articles for local newspapers and magazines."

Smith coughed. "She's better than the publications she writes for."

"You've read her stuff?"

Smith waved his hand and returned his attention to the manuscript on the desk. "I'm going to write about the events of my fifteenth year next," he stated, his tone cold and difficult to read.

Julia caught her breath. When Smith was fifteen, he'd been kicked out of his mother's house after his mother's (now ex) boyfriend admitted he "couldn't stand the kid." He'd threatened to leave Smith's mother if Smith didn't leave first. This meant Smith had spent six months mostly homeless, working odd jobs and getting by on the goodwill of others. When Smith had first shared these tidbits from his past, Julia had had to fight the urge not to throw her arms around him and take him home to be cared for properly.

Why was it that some people were born into such difficult circumstances? Why was life so often about the luck of the draw?

* * *

After Smith returned to his bedroom to get started on his new pages, Julia padded downstairs to find Anna and Violet at the kitchen table with mugs of steaming tea.

Violet was in the midst of a story about Dean when he was a kid, which made Anna laugh.

"You should have seen him, Anna," Violet said. "He was the most gorgeous little toddler, but he didn't know how to behave! You never would have thought that, meeting him later. He was such a gentleman."

With Julia in the kitchen, Anna perked up. "Mom! This is Violet. And Violet, this is my mother."

"Call me Julia," she said, reaching out to shake Violet's hand.

But before the handshake was over, Violet was on her feet, her smile enormous, her curls bouncing. She cradled Julia in her arms the way you might a friend you hadn't seen in a few years.

"I'm so pleased to be here!" Violet cried. "Anna has told me so much about you."

"Welcome," Julia said, taking a seat at the table. "How was your Christmas?"

Violet waved her hand, and Julia felt a jolt of grief. This was the first Christmas Violet had spent without her son. There were no words for how miserable it had probably been.

"Anna said you had just about every Copperfield under the sun here at the house," Violet said. "Dean just adored the family values of this little island. I could have seen him moving someplace like this to raise his son. He was never fond of the hustle and bustle of a bigger city. Even Seattle was too much for him, sometimes."

Violet spoke with the authority of a woman who still wanted to know her son better than anyone. She spoke as though Dean had known Anna was pregnant before his death. Anna's eyes flashed.

Julia poured herself a mug of tea and sat down with her daughter and the woman who should have been Anna's mother-in-law. Violet continued to smile at her. She was practically beaming. Julia guessed her cheeks were aching, that she was overdoing it, perhaps out of politeness.

"Anna was just telling me about how the pregnancy has gone," Violet said after a pause, her smile still plastered across her face. "She says it'll be any day now."

"You should see the presents Violet brought me," Anna said, puffing out her cheeks. "You went way too far!"

"It's not every day a woman becomes a grandmother for the first time," Violet assured her. "Your mother knows that, too."

Something in Anna's eyes gave Julia pause. "You're so generous. I'd love to see what you brought," Anna said.

For the past several months, Anna, Julia, Ella, Alana, and Greta had crafted a state-of-the-art nursery for Baby Copperfield, complete with a cradle, a rocking chair with a cushion, a diaper changing station, soft blue walls, and a rug that felt like clouds beneath your feet. More than a month ago, Anna and Julia had officially called it "finished." But when Anna led Julia and Violet back into the nursery this afternoon, Julia found it piled high with baby things they simply wouldn't use. Violet had bought additional items—another stroller, another cradle, and far more baby toys than anyone ever needed. Worst of all, the things she'd bought reeked of bad plastic. It made Julia cringe, thinking of Baby Copperfield in the midst of that terrible material. She and Anna had been purposeful about what they'd purchased.

But the look in Violet's eyes told Julia just how important these gifts were to her.

"As soon as you told me I could come out East to visit, I went on a shopping spree," Violet explained, picking up a dark yellow blanket and pressing it against her chest. "It reminded me of being a young mother twenty-five years ago, buying little things for baby Dean. Gosh, it breaks my heart to think about it." She blinked back tears.

Anna gave Julia a look that meant everything would be okay, and they would get rid of the new stuff in due time. But right now, they had to uphold Dean's love for his mother and his mother's love for his baby. It was the proper thing to do.

Not long afterward, Violet confessed she was tired after her two-day drive and retired to her bedroom to nap. They walked her down the hall, chatting about things that immediately fled Julia's mind. Before Violet closed the door, Julia thought she spotted four large suitcases stacked against the wall. Her eyes widened, even as she raised her hand to say goodbye. Anna took Julia's hand and guided her down the hall and upstairs to her bedroom, where she closed the door behind them and whispered, "I think she plans to stay forever."

Julia winced and crossed her arms over her chest. "Did she say anything?"

Anna dropped onto the bed and sighed toward the ceiling. "I mean, I thought she still had a job to get back to," she began, "but apparently, she quit last summer."

"I imagine the grief made it too difficult for her."

Anna nodded and swallowed. "She kept telling me how happy she is to be a part of my baby's life. And I can't push her away, you know? We both lost Dean. And I don't want her to think I don't honor his memory."

Julia sat on the bed beside Anna and collapsed onto the mattress, making it shake. Anna chuckled lightly.

"Nobody thinks you're not honoring Dean," Julia said quietly, taking Anna's hand.

Anna squinted. "But it's true that I've forgotten things about him. Little things."

"You've had a lot on your mind. You're growing a baby."

Anna raised her shoulders. Julia felt the heaviness of Violet's visit, how loaded it was for Anna. She resolved to make it easier on her.

"We'll do everything we can for Violet," Julia said tenderly.

Anna turned her head, and her eyes flashed. "I can't help but think about Baby Copperfield. About what it would be like to lose him twenty-four years from now." Fear overtook her face, and Julia squeezed her hand harder.

"As a mother, you'll never stop worrying," Julia said, her heart shattering. "It's just something you'll have to get used to."

Anna winced and turned her head back to gaze up at the ceiling. She sighed. "This is Violet's home for as long as she wants it. I'm sure we'll get used to each other. And I'm sure her husband will want her to come home soon."

"Right," Julia agreed. "Have you spoken to him?"

"Not at all," Anna said. "But Violet said he wants to come out to meet the baby in January. So I guess we'll have another guest at The Copperfield House soon."

Chapter Five

It was the second week of January. Anna checked her phone's pregnancy app—she was just a week and a half away from her due date so after stages of being the size of a walnut, an avocado, and a tiny melon, the baby was now the size of, well, a human baby. She sizzled with expectation and fear, even as acid reflux made her stomach and chest burn. She tried to cheer herself up, imagining her little baby with a full head of curly hair peering up at her.

There was a knock on her bedroom door. Anna gritted her teeth, already knowing who it was. It was confirmed a second later.

"Anna? Honey? I brought you a smoothie!" Violet's voice rang through her head like a gong.

Anna rubbed her eyes and put her feet on the floor beside her bed. "Come on in!"

It had been this way ever since Violet's arrival. It seemed like Anna never had a spare moment to herself, that Violet was perpetually on the other side of the door, or around the corner, or asking to make plans. She kept saying she wanted to form the "mother-daughter" bond they hadn't been allowed to have due to Dean's death. "Dean wanted to marry you," she'd said. "And just because it didn't happen doesn't mean I don't think of you as a daughter-in-law."

It was clear she was lonely. But Anna's patience was running thin.

Violet popped into Anna's bedroom with a mango-strawberry smoothie and placed it on Anna's bedside table, grinning broadly. She wore a pair of light green yoga pants and a zip-up sweatshirt, and her hair was tied into a tight ponytail that straightened out her eyebrows.

"Good morning, beautiful Anna!" Violet said, hurrying toward the window to draw back the drapes and let the January light in. She'd read somewhere that natural light was good for the fetus. This was yet another on her very long list of things to do for "baby's health" during the ninth month of pregnancy, all of which she'd attempted to cram into the past two weeks. Anna felt claustrophobic.

"Hi," Anna said, taking a sip of the smoothie and trying to remind herself that this situation wasn't forever. Violet would go back to Ohio. Eventually. "That tastes amazing. Thank you."

Violet beamed and wrapped her hands behind her back. "I thought we could get mani-pedis today. Don't worry. I looked it up, and it's a myth that you can't get mani-pedis while pregnant!"

Anna winced. In her normal life, manicures and pedicures weren't her thing. She wasn't a girly girl and instead considered herself an adventurer or a creative type.

"Besides," Violet was saying, "you're going to want

fabulous nails when the baby comes. Photos of the baby will feature your hands. Remember that."

Anna remembered Dean saying that his mother was slightly high-maintenance. She wasn't sure how she'd forgotten that before telling Violet to stay in The Copperfield House for as long as she wanted. She felt on the brink of losing her mind.

Anna asked Violet for a bit of time before they left for mani-pedis. She showered and sat on her bed, staring into space as her hair dripped across her shoulders. Around her, The Copperfield House was vibrant, with numerous footsteps shaking the ancient bones of the place. It sounded like Scarlet was still around—a surprise since she spent so much time in Manhattan. But Anna remembered now that Scarlet had just graduated from NYU in December. Maybe she planned to stick around the island for a little while. Maybe she needed time to think about what was next.

Anna texted her cousin with questions.

> ANNA: Hey! You're still here?

> SCARLET: Definitely! I'm still not sure about grad school, and Dad and I have another idea for a documentary.

> ANNA: So you'll be here for a while?!

> SCARLET: At least until May.

> ANNA: Ahh! Why didn't anyone tell me?

> SCARLET: (laughing-crying emoji) I don't know! You've been out and about since I got here.

> SCARLET: When are we going to hang out?

Anna chewed her lower lip and furrowed her brow, cursing the fact that Violet had pre-arranged her day without asking her. All she wanted was to sit on the back porch with Scarlet and gossip, just as they'd done all summer long. As Anna's belly had grown, Scarlet had dated her way across the island, tending to her own broken heart and telling Anna all about it. Sometimes, she'd even brought Anna along on her adventures. The parties had been necessary distractions, helping Anna pretend she was just a normal twenty-four-year-old woman.

Anna waddled downstairs to find Violet dressed in a coat and hat. Aunt Alana was perched behind her, poring over a magazine across her lap. A long time ago, Alana had worked as a fashion model, and she still liked to peruse magazines to keep abreast of the latest clothing trends.

"Hey, Aunt Alana," Anna stuttered. "Do you want to get mani-pedis with us?"

Alana would have normally jumped at that chance, but as she raised her head, her eyes glossed across Violet, taking stock of her. Violet had done little to make friends at The Copperfield House in the two weeks since she'd come to Nantucket. Anna had the sense that nobody trusted her—although she couldn't imagine why. Violet was just a lonely woman.

"I have plans later, unfortunately," Alana said. "Jeremy wants to meet for lunch."

"Too bad," Violet said, although she didn't sound upset about it at all. She wanted Anna all to herself.

A Winter's Miracle

When Anna opened the front door, she found the porch laden with cardboard boxes. Violet shrieked with happiness.

"I was hoping they'd get here in time," she said, scrambling to bring them inside.

Anna's heart sank. Violet's initial contribution to the nursery had doubled or tripled since her arrival. The nursery now looked like a hoarder's nest. It was hard to believe The Copperfield House featured such a trashy room. She had no plans to bring her baby inside, not until she could figure out a way to clean it up.

"Violet." Anna tried for the hundredth time as Violet released baby equipment from the boxes, tearing through the tape. "You're doing too much for me."

Violet smiled as though she'd won an award. "Nothing is too much for my grandson."

Anna forced herself through the mani-pedis, making small talk with the nail technician until Violet completely took over their conversation. This was a habit of Violet's—talking about her husband, her previous jobs, and her timeless memories in a way that completely obliterated anyone else's stories. The nail technician seemed accustomed to this. She popped another strip of gum into her mouth and finished Anna's toes as though she couldn't hear.

After Anna's fingernails dried, she picked up her phone and texted Scarlet.

> ANNA: Give me an excuse to get away. Anything.

> SCARLET: Um?

> SCARLET: Let's see.

> SCARLET: I need your help writing a pitch for a documentary company. Something like that.

> ANNA: Perfect.

> SCARLET: Meet on the back porch?

> ANNA: I'll be there in an hour.

Anna returned her phone to her pocket and smiled at Violet. "Thanks again for this awesome idea."

Violet waved her hands, showing off her lime-green nails. "It's a pleasure, honey. Really. These are the last 'easy' days of your life, you know. I want to make sure you're using your freedom."

Anna winced. When Violet said stuff like that, it terrified Anna even more about the future.

"Listen," Anna began, wrinkling her nose. "You know my cousin Scarlet?"

Violet raised her shoulders. "I've met so many of your cousins. It's hard to keep track."

"Right." Anna laughed. "She's the oldest daughter of Quentin. The newscaster?"

Violet's eyes were illuminated. Everyone remembered Quentin Copperfield, who'd graced their screens on the nightly news for decades. Now that he'd quit, Anna had seen several islanders and tourists alike taking stock of him on the street, trying to remember where they knew his face from. Quentin laughed, telling the Copperfields he looked a little "rough around the edges" these days. "I certainly wouldn't fit TV anymore," he'd said with a laugh, simply because he'd let his hair grow longer and shaggier and no longer wore suits every day.

"Oh, yes. I remember Scarlet," Violet said. It could have been a lie.

"Well, she needs some help this afternoon," Anna said. "She and her father are putting together a new documentary, and they need to pitch it to a, um, production studio."

Anna wasn't entirely sure that was how things worked. She hoped Violet didn't know either.

Violet's eyes were saucers. "Everyone in your family is on the verge of a big break."

"I don't know about that." Anna swallowed the lump in her throat. "But I would like to help her. If I can?"

Anna hated that she was asking for permission. She forced a smile.

"Of course, honey," Violet said. "You take all the time you need."

Down below, where she knelt before her, Anna's nail technician finished her pinky toe with a quick gash of his brush. So often, Anna had missed the nail on that toe and accidentally painted her skin instead. Now, her toes looked immaculate in a dark blue with glitter. She imagined she wouldn't have time to paint her toenails for the next several years—not with a baby and then a toddler in tow. She thanked the technician profusely and tied her hair into a ponytail.

"It's nice to see a mother and daughter together," the nail technician said, eyeing Violet.

Violet's cheeks were cherry red, and she splayed her hand over her mouth. "Did you hear that?" she whispered to Anna. "She thinks I'm your mother!"

As Violet and Anna walked back to the car, Violet babbled about this and that before actually saying something of interest. "That younger man," she said as she buckled her seat belt. "I don't know what to make of him."

The other artists at the residency were in their forties and fifties, which gave Anna a clue as to whom she spoke of. "Smith?"

Violet raised her shoulders. "I saw him spill a bag of pasta the other day in the residency kitchen."

Anna turned to squint at Violet.

"He looked so upset," Violet said. "I thought he was going to scream. He made a fist and smashed it against his thigh." Violet imitated him, striking her own fist lightly against her leg as she adjusted herself in front of the steering wheel. "I wanted to step into the kitchen. To tell him not to worry about something as silly as pasta. You would have thought the world was ending."

Anna grimaced. "Smith's been through a lot. I don't think anything's easy for him."

"It's just pasta," Violet muttered as she eased the car out of the parking lot.

An hour later, Anna tiptoed down the hallway, the staircase, and through the living room and back hallway to find Scarlet on the back porch. Although the back porch was enclosed, it was usually about fifteen to twenty degrees chillier out there, and Scarlet had set up a space heater and carried several blankets in from the living room. An enormous platter of food sat on the table—crackers, hard cheeses, sliced vegetables, fresh bread, various kinds of dark chocolate, and she'd brought a pot of tea and two mugs. Anna's heart melted.

"Scarlet! It's too much!"

Scarlet scooped Anna into a hug and laughed. "For you, Anna, nothing is too much."

Anna tipped herself into the chair beside Scarlet, and Scarlet wrapped her lovingly in the softest blanket.

"I can't believe you're still here," Anna breathed as she settled in. "I imagined you off in Manhattan, having the time of your life."

Scarlet cackled and placed a square of cheese on a cracker. "The idea of going back to Manhattan right now literally freaks me out. That last semester was grueling. And besides. Now that Dad and Mom are building a new house down the water from here, these are the last months I'll ever really live at The Copperfield House."

Anna's heart panged with dread. "I guess that was always going to happen. We can't physically live under one roof forever."

"I'll be just down the water," Scarlet assured her, her eyes softening.

Anna grumbled and rubbed her temples. "I'm sorry. My emotions are all over the board. I have no control anymore. And being with Violet nonstop..." She sensed herself in dangerous territory.

"It's okay," Scarlet said quietly. "I mean, I think I know what you want to say."

The tightness in Anna's chest loosened. "Is everyone talking about it?"

"Grandma is generally outraged," Scarlet admitted. "She thinks you need more time to yourself. Aunt Alana and Aunt Ella think Violet has a loose screw."

"And my mother? What does she think?"

"She hasn't said anything in front of me," Scarlet said. "Which was tactically smart. Obviously, I'm not keeping their secrets to myself."

Anna laughed into her mug of tea so that steam rolled across the table. "I want her to be comfortable here."

"But you don't want her to be so involved with your life that you can't breathe anymore."

"Something like that," Anna said with a laugh. "Maybe it'll calm down after the baby comes."

"It might get worse," Scarlet said, wincing.

Anna filled her mouth with tea and set the mug back down.

Scarlet nibbled another square of cheese thoughtfully, her gaze out the window. A sharp blast of wind crashed against the porch, making the glass rattle in their panes. Anna wanted to know every thought she was having, every creative impulse she experienced. She wanted Scarlet to guide her back into the beauty and freedom of being a young twentysomething with still so much to lose.

"Now that you're back, are you diving back into Nantucket nightlife?" Anna asked.

Scarlet chuckled. "Why? You want to go out after the baby comes?"

"I don't think I'll be free for a while," Anna said with a laugh.

Scarlet looked deflated. "There's a party at a beach house this weekend. A few islander guys are throwing it and hosting a few local bands. It'll probably be run-of-the-mill, but I'll make an appearance, I guess." She chewed her lower lip. "I ran into that new guy in the residency yesterday. His first name sounds like a last name?"

"Smith," Anna said. Her heart jumped into her chest and then returned to its original position.

"Right. Anyway, I realized he was about our age, maybe slightly older, so I asked what brought him to The Copperfield House, what he's working on, that kind of thing."

Anna hadn't seen Smith have a conversation with anyone at The Copperfield House. "What did he say?"

"Just that he's working with your mom to write a memoir," Scarlet said. "And that he doesn't know anyone here. So I invited him to the beach party this weekend."

Anna's head was suddenly fiery with jealousy. She sipped her tea, imagining Scarlet and Smith laughing together around a firepit with a five-foot-tall flame. She imagined Smith touching Scarlet's back delicately and gazing into her eyes.

"I told him it would be good to meet people on the island," Scarlet explained, "since it sounds like he'll be here for the better part of a year. But he looked at me like I was an alien. He says he doesn't 'do' parties anymore, whatever that means."

And just like that, Anna's fiery jealousy dissipated. She took a piece of cheese and nibbled on the edge. "That's weird."

"Right?" Scarlet laughed. "He looked at me like I was crazy for asking."

"He keeps to himself." Anna shrugged.

"Yeah. But people who keep to themselves are doing it as self-protection, right?" Scarlet asked. "And I want him to know he doesn't have to protect himself around here. We're the Copperfields. We take care of each other and the artists who reside here." She set her jaw.

Anna remained bubbly in the wake of learning Smith didn't want to go to mundane Nantucket parties with strangers. He preferred to remain alone, only a few rooms away from hers, typing or writing notes or dreaming about his memoir. Something about this and his volatile moods intrigued Anna. Smith had begun to seem like a fictional character in an old-fashioned book. She wasn't sure if she'd ever get a handle on him. She wasn't sure if he'd ever fully reveal himself. And maybe that was the magic of knowing (or not fully knowing) Smith.

That night, Anna and Scarlet joined the other Copperfields for dinner. Violet grabbed the seat on the other side of Anna and made sure to fill her plate with extra vegetables and babble in her ear about everything she'd gotten up to since they'd returned from getting their nails done. She was considering another purchase for the baby—a gadget Anna had never heard of.

"The baby industry just makes things up, don't they?" Scarlet tried to joke from the other side of the table.

Violet glowered at her. "I just want to make sure my grandson has the best possible start."

Nobody knew what to say to that. Eventually, Quentin changed the subject, even as Violet continued to pepper information into Anna's ear. Anna's heart felt the shape and texture of a small stone.

It was around the end of dinnertime that the cramps began. Anna's forehead crinkled with worry, and she touched both sides of her pregnant stomach and filled her lungs. Midway through Violet's monologue, she interrupted her. "I think I'd better get to bed. You know how important sleep is for the baby."

Upstairs, Anna lay on the bed with her clothes on, focusing on her breathing. Slowly, the cramps dissipated, and the heaviness over her chest fell away. A part of her had thought the baby was on his way. A part of her had been ratcheted with fear.

Anna checked her phone. It had been two hours since she'd come into her bedroom for space, and in that time, Violet had texted her three articles and ten messages, none of which Anna was up to reading. Julia had written, too, saying: "I'm off to Charlie's tonight. Someone has to plan that wedding, I guess. Ha!"

Perhaps because she was a masochist, Anna pulled up her final correspondence with Dean. In it, Dean had still been pretending he wasn't surprising her on Orcas Island, that he wasn't going to propose. She'd thought he was home, safe, in Seattle rather than waiting for her in her hotel room. *"I miss you so much!"* she'd written. *"I wish you were here."* But the words seemed so light and frivolous now. Anna hadn't known what missing Dean was really like.

With the cramps gone, Anna decided to undress. She forced herself to her feet and wandered to her closet, where she stopped short. Something light along the dark sand had caught her eye. Stepping closer to the window, so near that her nose nearly touched the glass, she peered out to watch a golden retriever whisk across the sand, his paws nearly touching the froth from the waves. Behind him, Smith slinked after him, his hands shoved in his pockets.

Anna suddenly felt that they were the two loneliest people in the world. It was a shame they couldn't talk about it or that they insisted on being apart.

These were silly thoughts, maybe. But Anna had been around the block enough to know you had to follow your gut. Only minutes after Violet arrived in Nantucket, Anna had wanted to demand that she leave. Now, look at the state of things. She should have listened to her instincts.

Anna donned a coat, hat, mittens, and boots and tiptoed downstairs to the back porch. In her head, she practiced what she might say to Smith as a distraction from his anger and self-hatred. It couldn't be too cheesy.

Smith was too intelligent for something like that. And she liked the idea of him regarding her as a friend.

But as Anna pressed open the screen door between the porch and the beach, the hinges shrieked. Luka's ears pointed skyward, and he bounced back toward the house, eager to sniff Anna. Anna was now totally outside, and the late-night chill wrapped around her like a snake. She rubbed Luka's head, conscious that Smith's eyes were upon her. Assessing her. Remembering her from the time she'd fallen right here two weeks ago. He probably hadn't thought of her in a good light since.

"Hi," Anna said as Smith approached.

Smith's eyebrows were raised. He strode through the sand and snow, his hands shoved deep in his pockets and his dark hair flowing behind his ears. His winter hat only covered the top tips of them. Greta would have called that "flirting with disaster." She believed in being prepared for all weather, for any season.

Unlike other people, Smith's eyes didn't trace her pregnant belly or make her feel like nothing but a baby carrier. They remained locked on hers. "Hi."

Anna swallowed the lump in her throat. Out of nowhere, she was reminded of the first time she'd ever gone out with Dean. She hadn't known what to say. It had felt like her tongue was made of stone.

"It's nice out here this time of night. Cold. But perfect for, I don't know. For thinking, I guess," Anna said, then cursed herself for speaking of the weather. How boring was she?

Smith turned to follow her gaze out across the inky water. Just then, the clouds separated to reveal a sliver of the glowing moon.

"I've been doing most of my writing at night," Smith

said. "After everyone in The Copperfield House is asleep."

Anna was intrigued. "So this is the beginning of your workday?"

Smith raised his shoulders. "You could say that."

Anna remembered Violet's story, in which Smith had smashed his fist against his thigh over something as trivial as spilled pasta. Her eyes flitted over his thigh. She wondered if he'd bruised himself.

"And you?" Smith asked. "When do you do most of your writing?"

Anna's eyes widened. Had she told him she was a writer? Had her mother? It both troubled and excited her to hear he knew things about her. And it terrified her to realize he might have read something as silly as her Christmas market write-up. She'd always felt destined to be a better writer than that. She'd been wrong.

"I like mornings and nights," Anna said, her voice catching in her throat. "I'm a bit like my grandmother and a bit like my grandfather in that regard. In the afternoons, I like to daydream." She laughed.

Smith gave her a very faint smile. It was the first Anna had ever seen him. It was a thrill.

"You do come from an incredible line of artists," Smith offered, taking a small step toward her.

"It's intimidating," Anna agreed. "Both of my grandparents are writing novels right now. And my mother, well...she's up to her ears in other people's stories."

Smith winced. "Sometimes I don't know why she took a chance on me."

Anna felt immediately tender toward him. It wasn't every day that a man like Smith revealed such a sensitive piece of his heart. She had to fight the instinct to throw her arms around him and assure him everything would be all right.

"My mother says you're a brilliant writer."

Smith's cheek flinched. "And I say you're brilliant," he said. "But you're writing for the wrong publications. You're too good for them. I hope the right ones come along and scoop you up soon."

Anna's jaw dropped. Hearing her thoughts echoing in a stranger's voice was bizarre. "You read my stuff?"

But just then, a flash of pain wrapped around her lower stomach like a belt. Anna crumpled forward, crying out. The moon disappeared behind the clouds again, shrouding them in darkness. And as Smith moved toward her, his face was etched in fear.

Something was happening. A change was imminent. And Anna wasn't sure she was strong enough to face it.

Chapter Six

Julia was surprised to see a missed call from Smith on her cell. It was late, after eleven, and she'd just spent the better part of the past few hours up to her ears in wedding plans on Charlie's couch. Even still, Julia was no event planner. The pieces were still fragments and hardly coming together.

"What's up?" Charlie asked as he deposited two beer cans into his recycling bin, returned to the living room, and ruffled his hair. Their conversation about place settings and what food to serve now seemed hilariously frivolous.

"Smith called," Julia explained.

"He can wait till tomorrow, can't he?" Charlie asked, drawing his arms around her and cradling her close.

"He's nocturnal. He'll be asleep tomorrow."

"You can catch the little vampire when he wakes up," Charlie assured her, kissing her ear gently.

A shiver of desire raced down Julia's spine.

"You know what I keep thinking about?" Charlie asked.

"Hmm?"

"I keep thinking about our initial plans for our wedding," Charlie said. "Back when we were teenagers."

Julia's smile widened. "Didn't you want a cotton candy machine?"

Charlie cackled. "Did I?"

"You said you wanted it to be part carnival, part wedding," Julia teased.

"I don't remember that." Charlie shook his head.

"Okay. What do you remember?"

"I remember we wanted to rent a powder-blue convertible to leave the ceremony in," Charlie said. "And we were going to invite everyone across Nantucket for a big beach bonfire afterward. And that after the party, we planned to go skinny-dipping in the sound."

A blush crawled across Julia's cheeks. She imagined them as they'd once been—beautiful teenagers with their entire lives in front of them. If only they hadn't moved to Manhattan. If only Charlie's mother hadn't gotten sick, requiring him to leave Julia alone in the city. If only they'd been allowed this other reality.

But before she could answer, her phone buzzed with another call from Smith.

"This must be a heavy case of writer's block," Charlie quipped.

"I have to take it. He literally never calls." Julia rolled her eyes as she answered the phone. "Hey, Smith. What's up?"

Smith was breathing heavily, and his voice rattled through the speaker. "Julia? Um. I don't know how to tell you this."

Immediately, all of Julia's hair stood on end. "What's going on?"

Charlie unshackled his arms from around Julia and placed his hands on his hips. He was ready to take action, whatever she needed him to do.

"It's Anna," Smith continued breathlessly. "Her water broke. We're almost to the hospital. You need to come. Now."

A bell went off in Julia's head. Why was Smith with Anna? It didn't make any sense. She listened to herself sputter anxious questions and demand that Smith keep her updated until she got to the hospital. "Make sure she's all right," she blared. "Make sure she knows I love her and everything will be okay."

When Julia got off the phone, Charlie passed her coat, hat, and gloves across the room. He was already dressed in his. His eyes were stony and resolute.

"Why was Smith with Anna?" he asked as Julia flung her winter garments on.

"I have a million questions," Julia confessed. "But right now, I'm terrified. I need to get to the hospital ASAP." She pulled her hat over her ears. "You don't need to come, Charlie. I can drive myself."

Charlie squared his jaw. "If you think for a second I'm letting you go through that alone, you're wrong."

Julia couldn't suppress a laugh. She whisked across the living room and burrowed her face in Charlie's chest. God willing, she would be a grandmother in just a few hours. She had to stay strong, for Anna's sake.

Charlie drove them through sputtering snow. Lamps and car lights were a blur, whizzing around them like a nightmarish music video. Julia was too terrified to speak. Instead, she busied herself with texting her ex-husband, Rachel, and Henry with news of Anna's labor. It was already tomorrow in Beijing, and Jackson texted back right away.

> JACKSON: Tell her I'll call her as soon as she's up for it.
>
> JACKSON: Tell her I'm pulling for her.

It warmed Julia's heart that Jackson finally found a balance between loving his children and pursuing his career. Julia didn't have a place in his life anymore, and that was okay. Julia squeezed Charlie's hand between their seats just as Charlie eased into the drop-off area at the hospital. "Text me where you end up," Charlie said. "I can be in the waiting room as long as you need me. I'll bring a never-ending stream of coffee and sandwiches."

"You're a dream." Julia kissed him and pressed her weight into the door. She was inside the hospital in a flash, racing for the labor and delivery floor, her tennis shoes squeaking on the linoleum.

A receptionist within the labor and delivery wing directed Julia to room 332. Julia hurried around rushing nurses and panicked, wide-eyed fathers to hover outside her daughter's hospital room. There, she found Anna already in bed, wearing a hospital gown and squeezing Smith's hand to a bloody pulp. Smith was pale beside her, still standing. It was the first time Julia had seen him without Luka in tow.

And now, because Smith and Anna still hadn't seen Julia, Julia was allowed a brief glance into their dynamic.

"It's okay," Smith breathed to Anna. "Just keep holding my hand. Squeeze it as hard as you can until the pain passes."

Anna's face was as red as a cherry. She squeezed her

eyes shut and squealed with pain until the contraction passed. All the while, Smith echoed similar sentiments, making sure she knew she was safe and protected. Julia couldn't bring herself to interrupt until it was over.

Julia stepped into the room.

"Mom!" Anna was sweaty and smiling. "That was fast!"

Julia hurried over and kissed Anna on the forehead. "Charlie drove like a maniac."

Smith looked sheepish. He brought both hands behind his back as though he wanted to pretend he hadn't been holding Anna's.

"It was so scary, Mom," Anna admitted. "I had no idea it was coming. And now, I'm here. And my body is totally taking over."

"Did you tell Violet?" Julia asked.

Anna grimaced and shook her head.

"It's okay," Julia said. "We can call her when the baby's here."

Smith stood abruptly and wiped his sweaty palms on his black jeans. Julia had never seen him look so uncomfortable.

"You can head home, Smith," Julia said gently. "I can't thank you enough for being there when Anna needed you."

Smith was speechless. His eyes dropped toward Anna's, who held his gaze with a mysterious gravity. Julia couldn't remember ever having seen the two of them together. Smith had mentioned Anna's writing exactly once, but Julia had allowed herself to forget about it till now.

"Given what happened with my mother later," Smith began then, surprising Julia with his earnestness, "it's a surprise how lovingly she always told my birth story. It was the only time she ever really seemed like my mother. Or like anyone's mother."

Anna's eyes glinted. "What was it?"

Smith laughed gently, and his shoulders shook. "She was doing a cross-country trip," he said. "Hopping from here to there, doing the best she could to make a buck or get something to eat. She was eight months pregnant at the time, but she didn't show very much, and many of the men who helped her along the way didn't know she was pregnant at all."

"That hasn't been my experience at all," Anna quipped, her face scrunching. It looked like another contraction was on its way.

"My mother had started hitchhiking with a trucker," Smith said. A kind fellow but someone who did the bare minimum of driving per day and always ended up at a dive bar along the highway. Mom always said he was one of the nicer guys she traveled with. She never had to stand up to him or remind him to respect her. And when he got drunk, he always got sweeter rather than meaner, like my father. But I digress."

Julia had never heard Smith even mention his father. With the hospital lights shining on his face, he looked as though he sat in a cell, spilling his secrets.

"When Mom went into labor, she was at one of those highway bars outside of St. Louis," Smith went on. "The trucker was out of his mind, drunk, and very difficult to reason with. He couldn't understand why she had to go to the hospital right that minute. Mom always said he wanted to dance the night away to a jukebox. But Mom was adamant that she wanted me to be born safely. So when the trucker was distracted, Mom stole the keys from his pocket and raced out into the parking lot. She stole the eighteen-wheeler and drove it to the hospital! By the time the trucker tracked his truck down the next morning, I'd already been born. The trucker was hungover and soft around the edges, and he could do nothing but wish my mother well. He even gave her a one-hundred-dollar bill to get started with."

Smith laughed and wiped a tear from his cheek. Julia's heart opened at the story. This version of his mother was every bit the mother of his darker stories—reckless and borderline insane. But it had worked out differently in this tale. Smith had been born safely. She'd done everything in her power to make sure of it.

Julia could understand why the story was so dear to his heart. It was one of the only examples of his mother's love.

As Anna peppered him with questions, another contraction fully took hold, and she grabbed Julia's hand as though her life depended on it. Julia's fingers crunched together. She whispered loving words to her daughter, anything to get her through the dark cloud of pain. And when Anna emerged, they turned to find that Smith had slunk out of the hospital room.

"Where did he go?" Anna gasped as Julia filled a glass with water.

"I'm sure he wanted to get home, sweetie," Julia said. "You know how Smith is. He doesn't do well in public."

Anna sipped the water, her eyes ponderous. "That was quite a story," she whispered. "It made me realize I've never heard my birth story."

Julia remembered only bits and pieces of that fateful day: flashes of pain, Jackson hovering over her, urging her on, her body becoming a stranger unto herself. She'd been blisteringly frightened, going through labor without her own mother or either of her sisters. It felt like the world no longer had gravity. She'd ached to call them back home in Nantucket, yet she hadn't been strong enough to bridge the barrier between them. And when Anna had burst into the world, Julia had been so overwhelmed with responsibilities and love that she'd allowed years to drift by.

Chapter Seven

In hindsight, Anna would block out so much of her labor and delivery. This, she would read, was a coping mechanism—a way for her mind and body to prepare for another baby, should she ever want one. Years later, she would remember amorphous pain, her mother's hands, and the nurses bursting in and out to measure her or assure her of something that made little sense to her when she was this deep into the physical transformation. In some ways, the entire event felt like a horror movie. In others, it was the most rapturous fifteen hours of Anna's life.

When the contractions were hardly a minute apart, Anna's mother seemed to get up the nerve to ask the question that sizzled between them. "Why did Smith bring you to the hospital?"

"I was lucky he was there," Anna responded, wincing into another contraction. "I mean, can you imagine if I'd been alone?"

"But you weren't alone," Julia pointed out. "You were

at The Copperfield House. At any one time, more than ten people live there. All of them have licenses."

But Julia was too late. Anna huffed into another contraction, closing her eyes as a wave of pain flowed through her. Julia got the hint that Anna wouldn't reveal more, so she dropped it.

It wasn't like there was much to say, anyway. Being curious and slightly reckless, Anna had left her room to speak to Smith on the beach. It wasn't every day you decide to go flirt with a boy, only to have him take you to the hospital to deliver someone else's baby moments later. It was embarrassing. It was also a pretty good story.

Only twice did Julia find time to leave the hospital room for a cup of coffee and a bathroom break. As she sped through the waiting room, she spotted Charlie, Greta, Alana, Ella, and Scarlet, who had formed a circle around a box of donuts and many coffee cups. Flowers ladened the table, and balloons floated overhead. Everyone looked exhausted. Julia wondered if anyone had mentioned Anna's delivery to Violet on their way out of the house. She imagined Violet wandering aimlessly through The Copperfield House, wondering where everyone had gone. Perhaps it was up to Julia to contact her? But then again, she didn't want Violet's anxious energy around the hospital wing. She wanted Anna to deliver her baby in peace.

Around the corner and down the glistening white hall, Julia was surprised to find Smith curled around his cell phone, reading what looked to be an e-book. Julia's mouth was dry in surprise. All at once, the story of

Smith's mother stealing the eighteen-wheeler filled her mind. The publisher side of her brain ached to run over to him and tell him, "That deserves space in your memoir!" But maybe he already knew that?

Anna gave birth to a baby boy at three thirty that afternoon. Julia was the only other person in the room besides the doctor and a nurse. She had the remarkable privilege of welcoming her first grandchild and holding him only a few minutes after Anna held him for the first time. In her mind, she made a silent promise. *"I will protect you and love you forever."*

* * *

Anna named the baby Adam. She whispered it to him first, allowing him to try it on. And when it seemed to fit, she raised her chin to her mother and breathed, "What do you think?"

Julia touched the little boy's arm gently as her eyes filled with tears. "I love it, honey."

Throughout Anna's pregnancy, she'd created list after list of baby names, which she'd never shared with anyone. In another reality, she and Dean would have talked endlessly about baby names, having arguments about the best ones or pitching silly options. That had been the nature of their relationship.

With Dean gone, "Adam" had fallen from the sky and landed on one of her lists, striking her with its simplicity and its meaning. Adam had been the first man in Genesis. This suited her. After all, she and Adam would have to forge a new, Dean-less reality. They would have to be brave and strong, as the first Adam had been.

After little Adam had been a part of the world for

more than an hour, Anna drifted off to sleep. It was impossible to know how long she was out. But when she heard angry voices outside her door, her eyes burst open, and she turned over in bed, searching for Adam. These were the first hours they weren't connected physically, and that fact had formed a dull ache in her throat.

Nobody had told her how painful it would be once you were separated from your child.

It took a moment for Anna to realize who bickered outside the hospital door.

"She's exhausted. She needs her rest."

"But you have to understand," another voice barked, "I would have been here. I should have been here."

"We can't change that now." This, Anna realized, was her mother's voice. The other was Violet's. Her heart sank with recognition. Violet was brokenhearted that she hadn't been there for the birth.

Violet began to cry. Anna shifted up in bed, rubbing her eyes and getting eyeliner and mascara all over her fingers. When her mother appeared in the crack in the doorway, Anna waved and, before she lost her nerve, said, "Bring Violet in."

Julia stumbled and tilted her head. "Are you sure?" she mouthed. She knew more than anyone how Anna felt about Violet.

Anna nodded, trying to make herself feel serene and soft. Violet was just a grandmother, overwhelmed with new love and tragedy. She had to find a way to welcome her.

Violet was drying her cheeks of tears as she entered the hospital room. Her eyes grazed Anna's face before dropping down into the bassinet beside the bed, where the tiniest baby in the world slept soundly. Just as the doctor had said, Adam had been born with a full head of curly black hair, which now burst from the edges of his little winter hat. He was a miracle.

"My goodness," Violet whispered as she knelt beside the bassinet and peered inside. She shook her head as her eyes filled with another round of tears. "He looks just like Dean."

News of this shot through Anna's heart. She closed her eyes against a wave of feeling, terrified that she wouldn't be able to stop herself if she burst into tears.

"You can hold him," Anna whispered, "if you want."

Violet nodded and wrapped her arms around the tiny baby. As she nestled him to her chest, she sat gingerly and gazed at his face, his soft cheeks, his translucent eyelids. Anna had to continually remind herself that this baby was hers, that he was her responsibility forevermore, that he would one day grow up to learn stories of his father and look at Dean's photograph, looking for clues that he was his.

But he would be raised in The Copperfield House. He would be known as Copperfield rather than Carpenter. And that was sure to break Violet's heart.

When Anna told Violet his name was Adam, Violet nodded and said, "Dean would have approved." Anna wanted to take issue with that. Had Dean really told Violet what kind of names he would have selected for a child? She doubted it.

More likely, Violet had begun to construct another version of Dean, one that belonged to her rather than reality. It was only natural to do this after someone's untimely death. Anna had begun to do the same.

"Don't worry, Adam," Violet breathed as she cradled

the sleeping baby. "I'll teach you everything I know. And I'll protect you. Every day of my life."

Behind her, Julia rubbed her forehead with the flat of her palm and shifted her weight.

"Have you told your husband he has a grandson?" Anna asked, surprising herself.

Violet's eyes flickered. "Of course," she said. "He's just as over the moon as I am."

"When is he coming out to meet him?" Anna asked.

"Any day now," Violet affirmed. "He's just wrapping up a few things back home. And then, he'll run across the country to meet you, dear Adam. I can hardly wait."

After Violet returned to the waiting room, Julia collapsed into the chair beside Anna's bed and sucked her lower lip into her mouth. Anna considered making a joke about Violet, about how she'd thought she would never leave the hospital room. But a moment later, there was another knock on the door. Julia opened it to reveal Smith. Anna's heart burst in her chest.

"Smith!" Anna was surprised at the adrenaline that coursed through her body as he stepped into the hospital room. "What are you still doing here?"

"I left briefly," Smith explained, palming the back of his neck. "I had to feed Luka and take him for a walk."

Warmth flooded Anna's chest as she considered this man's commitment to his dog. It seemed proof of the goodness in him—a goodness he wasn't entirely willing to show anyone else.

Julia waved from the door. "I'm going to go talk to Charlie," she said, her eyes dancing from Smith to Anna and back. Her expression burned with curiosity. "Come get me if you need anything."

Julia closed the door, leaving Smith, Anna, and

Adam alone. Smith sat at the edge of the chair Julia had vacated and stared into the bassinet. He looked vaguely frightened of Adam, as though he hadn't actually considered that a real, live baby would be the result of all that pain from earlier. In some ways, Anna had felt the same.

"It's hard to believe we all came into the world like that," Smith said softly. "That we were all so small and helpless."

Anna's heartbeat quickened. Remembering Smith's birth story, she fought the urge to reach over and take his hand.

"But don't worry," Smith added before Anna could think of anything to say. "I won't put anything half as cheesy as that in my memoir."

Anna laughed in surprise. "I don't think it's cheesy."

"It's a boring fact," Smith protested. "We were all babies once upon a time. Writers across history have made that point again and again. It's banal."

Anna furrowed her brow, even as a smile played across her lips. She had the sudden sensation that she wanted Smith to remain at her bedside to argue about ideas and writing for the next several hours. Something about his presence made her brain quiver with ideas.

"But your story is specific to you," Anna pointed out. "And if your memoir is really a story about you and your mother..." She hoped he wouldn't get angry that she knew so much about his project. "Then isn't it essential to talk about the dynamic at the very beginning? Your helplessness? Your mother driving down a Midwestern highway in a stolen eighteen-wheeler?"

Smith's smile widened, and dimples formed on both cheeks. Anna had never seen him like that. It was hard to imagine him smiling much at all, but the effect wasn't alarming. It was nourishing.

"She was really something," Smith said thoughtfully.

"She sounds strong," Anna said. She didn't add stronger than me, although she felt it was true. There was no way in heck she could have driven an eighteen-wheeler to the hospital during the throes of labor.

"That's just one of many definitions of her," Smith agreed, his smile fading bit by bit.

In his bassinet, Adam groaned, then wailed, trying out his vocal cords, learning to cry. Fearful, Anna asked Smith to bring back her mother, who, she hoped, would know what to do. But, even as Smith fled down the hallway, it was strange how the mothering instinct took hold of her. One minute, she was fascinated with Smith's story, doubled over with flirtation and intrigue. And the next, it was as though Smith wasn't anywhere nearby at all. Her body and mind were programmed to help Adam. And that was just the way things had to be.

But as Adam fell back asleep in Anna's arms ten minutes later, Anna returned her thoughts to Smith, whose mother, in the wake of his birth, hadn't found herself with any real mothering instincts at all. It terrified her, imagining mothers across the world without the innate care required for their baby's health.

"You're already a natural," Julia said, stroking Anna's hair as though she'd heard Anna's anxious thoughts rolling around her head. "This is day one of the rest of your life. And you're doing great."

Chapter Eight

Last April

Violet found it ridiculous that she was required to hold a wake. Only a few days ago (days that seemed unreal and totally nightmarish), her darling son, Dean, had fallen off a cliff on Orcas Island and passed away. Now, for social reasons that dictated how you acted and how you were seen by your peers, she was stationed at the kitchen counter, making one hundred and fifty tiny sandwiches with tuna, roast beef, or roasted tomato with cheese and checking on her wine, beer, and spirits order, which was set to arrive within the hour. She hadn't cried since last night, alone in her bedroom, and she'd begun to ask herself if she'd run out of tears. Maybe you were only allowed to do so much mourning before something inside you broke.

Midway through her seventy-fifth sandwich, Violet heard footsteps in the living room. She retreated from the counter to find her husband, Larry, still in his boxers and a ratty T-shirt, a collapsed heap on the couch. He hadn't showered in several days, and she could smell his body odor from the doorway.

Violet had once read a novel in which a married couple had fallen more in love in the wake of a family member's death. She'd considered it romantic, the idea that two people could come together and build each other up in their times of darkness. But now that she and Larry had suffered a traumatic loss of their own, Violet wasn't sure how something like "falling in love" would ever be possible again. Larry could hardly look her in the eye.

Even before this happened, Violet and Larry didn't have the most passionate of marriages. They ate meals together; they watched television together. They complained about their city's politics and the ever-rising gas prices together. But now, Violet suspected something had irrevocably broken between them. There was no repairing it.

On the drive to the funeral that afternoon, Violet babbled softly about Anna, mostly to herself and whoever wanted to listen. Anna was Dean's girlfriend, the young woman who'd dragged him into the woods of Orcas Island. If it wasn't for her, Dean would still be alive today. Violet felt that fact deep in her bones.

"I don't know how I'll be able to look at her," Violet was saying of Anna. "I don't even know why she feels the need to come. The two of them hardly knew each other. They dated for less than a year."

"They were engaged, Violet," Larry shot back, his tone harsh. "They were planning a life together."

Violet wanted to protest, to remind Larry that young people got engaged and broke up all the time. It was just a matter of passing the days away for them.

Violet had no memory of the funeral. Even as she sat

A Winter's Miracle

in the pew and listened to the dull babble of the pastor, she sensed the words flowing in, through, and out of her without her making sense of them. She was reminded of being a teenager in science class, blinking up at the teacher, pretending to listen. How many hours of her life had she wasted like that?

After the funeral, Dean's girlfriend told her she didn't plan to come to the wake—that she needed to return home to Nantucket. Violet allowed herself to get angry about it for a moment; she felt it flash across her chest. But when the anger passed, she felt only gratefulness that Anna got the hint and headed out. She didn't want to see Anna lurking through the crowd at Dean's family home. Anna was the last person to see Dean alive. *If this was a thriller novel*, Violet thought, *Anna would have been the unassuming murderer*. The one they took down at the very end. "It was her all along!"

At the wake, Violet tried to joke about this to her sister, who gave her a look that told her this was inappropriate to say.

"We know you're going through a hard time, Vi," her sister said. "But be careful what you say to other people right now, okay?"

Violet got the hint. Nobody actually cared about her state of mind. Rather, they cared about how her grief looked to outsiders. And if she wasn't grieving "correctly," then they wanted to give her a wide berth. Acting differently, especially in a place like Ohio, wasn't rewarded. You had to fit the mold.

As Violet wandered through the wake, saying hello to people and trying her best to look the part, she couldn't help but live through hundreds, if not thousands, of memories of Dean. Wasn't it right here, on this Turkish rug, that Dean had taken his first steps? Hadn't Dean burst through the front door thousands of times, throwing his backpack to the ground before he grabbed a snack in the kitchen? And there, crying in the corner, was Dean's high school girlfriend, whom Violet had never really liked. She'd never seemed good enough for Dean. Now, though, Violet wished Dean would just have married her when he'd had the chance. He never should have run off to Seattle. He should have stayed here, where it was safe.

Miraculously, Larry had showered, shaved, and donned a suit for the funeral and wake. He was soft-spoken yet frequently smiling, walking through the crowd and greeting guests. He looked as though he'd just stepped from the pages of a fashion magazine. Violet thought this was yet another hardship of getting older as a woman. Men in their mid-forties gave off waves of confidence; they looked good when they threw on a suit and put a little gel in their hair. By contrast, Violet had to go through the wringer of face creams, Botox, Pilates, perfumes, and makeup in order to prove she cared about herself. And even then, she was a woman in her forties—which frankly made her less desirable than ever.

It was inappropriate to think about such things at her son's wake. But it was also hard not to remember her own demise now that her son was gone. Time was so fleeting.

Violet returned to the kitchen to restock a bucket of ice. Her sister scampered after her, saying, "Let me do that, Vi. Sit down." But didn't these people understand? Violet felt better and more useful when she had something to do with her hands. She was a mother. She was accustomed to being busy.

With her sister busy with the ice bucket, Violet let her hands fall to her sides and gazed out the side window, which faced west. The gorgeous day in April reminded her of Dean's old baseball games. Her heart felt crunched.

And then, Violet realized something was behind the tree in the side yard.

Vaguely curious, but only because it was a welcome distraction, Violet tiptoed across the room and peered out the window. On either side of the thick maple trunk, she could make out elbows, knees, and flashing hair. It looked to be a man and a woman, both of them dressed up. It stood to reason they'd been part of the wake. Violet cursed them for feeling free enough to enjoy the beautiful evening. She remembered Anna driving across the continent and heading back to Nantucket toward her family. Violet wondered if she would ever feel that freedom again, the wind in her hair.

That was when her husband stepped out from the other side of the tree. Larry glanced to his right and spread his hand over the top of his gelled hair. He looked as though he was making sure nobody had seen him. Violet's heart stopped. Larry took another step forward before a woman's hand wrapped around his arm and tugged him back behind the tree. They disappeared for a moment, drawing so close together that it wasn't hard to imagine what they were doing. Violet was gutted to the core. What kind of man cheated on his wife at their son's wake? It was the sort of scandal that people in Ohio would never get over. Violet had the insane impulse to jump into the living room and announce it to their guests.

Behind Violet, her sister began to talk about what was next in order for Violet to make a "better transition," whatever that meant. "A support group meets at the community center," she said. "And I'm friends with a grief therapist. We do yoga together. You really have to check her out. She says some of the most profound things to me over, like, lunch."

All the while, Violet's eyes remained glued to the tree. She didn't want to miss it when they inevitably walked out and returned to the party. Like watching a car crash, she needed to know how bad this was.

"Are you listening to me?" Violet's sister asked.

"Mm-hmm," Violet returned.

And then, it happened. Larry emerged, adjusting his suit jacket over his shoulders and glancing back to smile adoringly at the woman behind the tree. As he strode through the fresh spring grass, a woman in a pale blue dress headed in the opposite direction, away from the party. It didn't take Violet long to figure out why.

The woman was Hazel Applewood.

Immediately, Violet twisted away from the window and collapsed against the wall, nearly toppling the calendar to the floor. Her sister ogled her a large spoon over a container of potato salad, which she planned to spoon into the serving bowl. "Honey? Are you okay?"

How could Violet answer this question?

It was true that Violet hadn't thought of Hazel Applewood in probably eight years. Just as she'd promised she would, Hazel had left town, gotten another job, and fled their lives. Violet had locked the story of Hazel in the back of her mind, calling it "things better off forgotten." But she was back. And the timing couldn't have been worse.

Violet filled a glass with water and drank it in a single gulp. Other members of her extended family entered the kitchen to see how they could help, and Violet's sister put them to work, pointing and ordering. Violet grabbed a lemon cookie from a tray and ate it slowly, trying to relish the flavors of the decadent textures. Her stomach rumbled with hunger pains. This was the only food she'd given herself all day.

Violet floated upstairs and spread herself like a sea star on the bed she'd shared with her husband since their marriage at age twenty. Like almost all of their friends, they'd been high school sweethearts. They'd had a plan until Hazel Applewood had come along to squash it.

Violet still remembered the first time she'd seen Hazel. It had been ten years ago at parent-teacher night at Dean's high school. Dean had been a freshman at the time, enrolled in Hazel's biology class. Hazel was in her late twenties, a brand-new teacher with bright-eyed optimism about the ways teaching could dramatically alter her students' outlook on life. She spoke poetically about this during parent-teacher night in a way that made the fathers rapt with attention, and their wives roll their eyes. Still, Violet admitted to the other wives it was nice to meet a teacher who genuinely cared about their children's well-being. "She wants the best for them."

Violet had been tremendously busy at the time. She'd owned her own accounting business, driven Dean from place to place, belonged to several book clubs, and always had food on the table for dinner. It made sense why she hadn't suspected anything at first. After all, Larry had made it to most dinners. He'd attended almost all of Dean's games. He'd even been around to help Dean with his homework here and there.

The first hint had been the perfume. She'd smelled it on his button-down, like a bad cliché, and she'd nearly vomited with the realization. She'd never worn that perfume before.

Immediately, she called her sister. "This is what men do," her sister had assured her quietly. "He'll probably get over it and come back to you."

Violet had been flabbergasted. She was just supposed to sit at home and wait for Larry to get over his fling? She was just supposed to put food on the table, wash everyone's clothes, go to work, come home on time, and pretend nothing was wrong?

The doctors had called what happened next a "partial nervous breakdown." Perhaps due to grief, Violet didn't remember most of it. Her secretary had called her accounting clients to ask for a month's extension. Her sister had come over to cook for the kids. Violet had spent a few nights in a hospital with white walls, her brain on the edge of an abyss.

Violet's husband was asked to attend one of her therapy sessions in the hospital, where Violet revealed what she'd learned about "the woman." All the blood had drained from Larry's face. At first, he'd spat accusations, telling the therapist that he was in a "loveless marriage." And then, when Violet hadn't risen to the argument, Larry had broken down, saying, "It's the kid's science teacher."

When the therapist asked Larry if he planned to leave, Larry looked at Violet with large, soulful eyes. Within them, Violet had seen their decades of love, their endless stream of memories. And she'd known, in her heart of hearts, that he had no plans to leave her, even if he fantasized about it sometimes.

Besides, he felt too guilty.

And so, ten years ago, Larry had returned. But news of Larry and Hazel's relationship had spread across town. Hazel had been demonized, and she'd requested to transfer to a nearby town. Within the year, Violet had allowed herself to forgive and forget.

After the wake quieted beneath her and everyone but a few returned home, Violet listened to Larry's familiar footfalls as he came upstairs. She remembered herself all those years ago in the hospital and wondered why she'd resolved to continue to love Larry forever. Had it been a lack of imagination? Had she forgotten that she had one finite life?

Didn't she respect herself more than this?

Larry appeared in the gray shadows of the bedroom. He removed his suit jacket and lay on the bed beside Violet, staring at the ceiling. Just as he had ten years ago, he smelled of Hazel's perfume. Violet waited for the familiar anger to swell in her chest. It didn't.

"So here you are," Larry said finally.

"Here I am."

Larry rubbed his forehead. "Your sister's a trip, you know that?"

Violet remained quiet. They'd had this conversation many times, poring over the details of Violet's sister's inability to show compassion and respect in conversation. But Violet's sister had been there for her through thick and thin. Meanwhile, Larry had been in the side yard, plotting his escape.

Violet propped herself up on her elbow and turned to face Larry. This close to him, the air was thick with the perfume, which sizzled in her nostrils.

"When did it start again?" Her voice was firm yet not accusatory.

Larry frowned, and that familiar wrinkle deepened between his eyebrows. Violet knew his face so intimately; she knew every nook and cranny; she could practically envision how it would age into the future. But she wasn't sure she would be around for it.

"Just tell me," Violet said quietly. "I'm not angry. I'm too brokenhearted."

Larry blinked several times as though he wished he were dreaming and wanted to wake up. And then, he said, "After Dean passed away, she called. She wanted to meet." Larry stuttered. "I was so broken. I needed to talk to someone."

Violet nodded, urging him to go on. She remembered that when they'd first received word of Dean's death, she'd locked herself in the bathroom and refused to come out. She and Larry hadn't been able to give each other any comfort. She'd suddenly felt he was a stranger. Or maybe she'd felt that way all along.

"I went to see her," Larry went on, "and I realized how much I've missed her over the years."

Violet nodded. She tried to pretend that Larry was an acquaintance, telling her a story of his long-lost love. She tried to find happiness for him.

"You've lost so much time together," Violet said.

Larry flinched. "It's not that I regret any of our time together." He said it as though he knew he had to.

"Now that Dean's gone, we can't pretend anymore," Violet assured him. Each word felt like a knife through her heart. "We have to build lives that will make us happy."

Dean's eyes glistened. He reached over and took her hand in his. Violet guessed this would be the last time they ever touched. There would be no more casual hand holding. There would be no more kisses before they left home.

"I tried to love you as best as I could," Violet offered, her voice breaking.

"Dean wouldn't want us to be miserable," Larry said.

This was the final wound. Violet closed her eyes, trying to come to terms with the fact of her life: that her husband had been miserable when married to her and that for ten years, he'd longed to be with someone else.

Downstairs, someone dropped something in the kitchen. It sounded as though glass scattered across the floor. Violet remained motionless on the bed, listening as other people busied themselves, cleaning up the mess of her life. It was impossible to know where her story would guide her next. But she imagined herself completely alone, without anyone to come home to. And she tried to make peace with the idea that her life, as she'd once known it, was officially over.

Chapter Nine

Present Day

It wasn't such an uncommon thing for a new mother to struggle with breastfeeding. Just because it had come easily for Julia twenty-four years ago didn't mean Anna and Adam would immediately be up for the task. Doctors, nurses, and specialists all agreed—it would be all right. Julia tried to instill in her daughter a level of confidence, to remind her that "fed was always best." But Anna had read too many articles on the internet. She now regarded herself as a "failure" each time she requested time with the lactation consultant. And Adam was only two days old.

"You're not a failure, honey," Julia reminded her. "You love and care for your baby. You're here. That's all that matters."

Not for the first time, Julia thought of Smith's mother, who'd created a poisonous atmosphere for growing up and instilled in her child the belief that he wasn't good enough, that the world was cruel. Anna would never do that to Adam. She wouldn't even dream of it.

Unsurprisingly, Violet made sure to be at the hospital when it was time to take Anna and Adam home. As was her custom, she stuck her nose where it didn't belong, urging Anna to "keep working" at breastfeeding.

"Breast is always best," Violet said, her eyes wide. "I breastfed my children. And I know for a fact they weren't as sick as my sister's children, who were all fed from the bottle. And don't you think formula is poisonous? Unnatural?" She wrinkled her nose.

"They've done so many studies," Julia chimed in for what felt like the fifteenth time. "There are plenty of amazing formula options on the market. You have to do what's best for you and Adam and no one else. Okay?"

But Anna looked disgruntled and weary. She'd dressed in a big sweatshirt and a pair of leggings, and she held baby Adam with arms that didn't yet look comfortable with the task. Pregnancy was hard enough, Julia remembered. It was easy to forget that the real "hardships" came afterward—especially when other parents decided to share unsolicited parenting advice. The fact that this parenting advice came from the grieving mother of Anna's dead fiancé did not make things easier.

"Let's get you home," Julia said. "Everyone's anxious to see you both."

Julia wheeled Anna from the hospital with Violet hot on her heels. At the exit, Charlie sat idling in Julia's SUV, in which they'd already attached the baby car seat. Gingerly, Julia helped Anna slip Adam into the car seat as Violet attempted to help from a distance. "Watch his chin!" she cried. Anna and Julia made momentary eye contact, both annoyed.

In the car, Julia and Anna sat on either side of Adam's car seat in the back as Violet babbled up front. To Julia's surprise, Anna texted her from two feet away.

ANNA: She hasn't mentioned leaving Nantucket yet, has she?

JULIA: Unfortunately, no.

ANNA: I don't know what to do.

ANNA: She's ruining new motherhood for me.

ANNA: Then again, I'm underslept, in pain, and very cranky. I'm sure I'm just being dramatic.

JULIA: I'll do my best to create a perimeter. And there will be so many people at The Copperfield House to distract her. I hope.

Scarlet had hung a "WELCOME HOME, ANNA AND ADAM" banner between two posts on the front porch. Although it was mid-January, it was strangely warm, with a balmy, fiftyish-degree wind sweeping off the sound. Several Copperfield members were stationed across the porch, waving frantically as Anna walked slowly toward them, grinning from ear to ear. The crowd parted to allow Anna inside, where the rest of the family members spilled through the living room. Greta had set up a long table with plenty of snacks and red velvet cake with cream cheese frosting. On the far end of the table was a framed photograph of Anna and Adam—the first that had ever been taken. In it, Anna looked stunning and mystified, as though she couldn't believe she'd just done what she'd done.

Julia helped get Anna situated in one of the cushioned chairs. The baby slept soundly in his carrier beside

A Winter's Miracle

her as Copperfield members approached to squeak with happiness.

"He's so cute, Anna!" Scarlet cried. "I don't think I've ever seen a better baby."

Beside her, Scarlet's mother, Aunt Catherine, nodded serenely. "Congratulations, Anna."

Greta streamed through the crowd, looking effervescent, her white hair shining. Although she'd already met Adam on his first day in the hospital, she exclaimed that he was already slightly different. "They grow up so quickly, Anna. Blink, and they change."

This was Greta's first great-grandchild, and she prompted the rest of the Copperfield clan to celebrate accordingly. "Everyone! I've made enough food to feed a small army. There's plenty of wine, beer, and spirits in the kitchen. Quentin, can I trust you to make cocktails? It's a party!"

Even Alana gushed over the baby, sitting cross-legged beside his carrier. "I almost never regret not having kids," she said. "But little Adam is something special."

Anna's initial annoyance over Violet in the hospital had given way to joy. She told everyone who would listen about how wonderful Julia had been as her birth partner and described just exactly how her heart had burst open when she'd first held Adam. Everyone listened intently, grateful to see the happiness reflected in Anna's eyes. Everyone had worried about her. Everyone had pulled for her. And everyone prayed that Dean's death wouldn't be the nail in Anna's coffin—that she would find a way to keep going. Adam was proof that time always healed.

The door between the residency and the family house opened to reveal Smith. He took one look at the massive family huddled together, eating cake and drinking wine, and froze. Several emotions played out over his face. One of them was regret. But a split second later, Greta ushered him into the house, urging him to grab a plate.

Julia checked her phone for the time. It was only one thirty—hours before Smith normally got himself out of bed to write. And she had a hunch she knew why.

"Welcome back," Smith said as he ambled through the crowd to reach Anna.

Anna's eyes lit up. "Smith. Hey." She shifted to the edge of her seat and stood so that her and Smith's noses were just a few inches from one another. Julia forced her gaze away. Although she didn't entirely approve of whatever bubbling attraction this was, she could do nothing about it. And she had to assume it would fizzle out, anyway.

"Look at this, Julia."

A phone was suddenly shoved in her face. Frowning, Julia turned to find Violet beside her, her lips in a paper-thin line. On the screen of her phone was an article called "Why Doctors Recommend Breast Milk Above All." Slowly, Julia shoved the phone to the side and said, "Can I talk to you, Violet? In the kitchen?"

Violet followed Julia down the hallway. Greta bustled past them, carrying an enormous platter of French cheeses. "Anna can eat brie again!" she called.

In the kitchen, Julia asked Violet to sit down. Her stomach bubbled with rage and annoyance, which she tried to quell. Violet sat and crossed her ankles.

"Isn't it wonderful that he's home?" Violet said.

Julia's smile was strained. "It really is. I know Anna's so happy to start the next chapter of her life. And I'm excited to help her."

"Me too."

Julia winced and dropped into the chair across from Violet. Above everything, she had to protect her daughter and her grandson.

"I think we need to talk," Julia began.

"Okay?"

"It's been, um, so nice to have you here," Julia went on. "But if you're going to stay a little bit longer, I think we need to build a united front to help Anna. We need to work together."

Violet's gaze darkened, and she crossed her arms over her chest. "I'm here as an advocate for Dean. I know what he would have thought was best for his son."

Julia struggled not to roll her eyes at that one. Dean had been twenty-five at the time of his death. He'd probably never held more than five babies, let alone had opinions about how to raise one.

"And I know Anna appreciates that," Julia said delicately. "But she's also going through a very strange and traumatic time."

"I can't imagine hanging around that angry young man will help her," Violet said, referring to Smith.

Julia sighed and rolled her shoulders back. "Can we just agree to be patient with Anna right now? And not pester her too much about things like breastfeeding?"

Violet set her jaw and just barely twitched her head forward into a nod.

"Great," Julia said, although she wasn't sure she could trust Violet. "That reminds me. Is your room big enough to host you and your husband when he comes out? My mother said we can always move you to another room."

This was a white lie. Greta hadn't suggested anything.

"Oh. Um." Violet bit her lower lip. "I'm sure it'll be big enough. Larry and I don't need much."

In the next room, little Adam squawked. This was followed by Bernard's booming voice. "He's already singing! He's a Copperfield!" he cried.

Violet's cheeks were pale. All at once, it was as though her mood crashed in on itself, and her shoulders drooped. Big bags hung beneath her eyes.

It occurred to Julia that Violet's moods were erratic. That she could never count on them sustaining for longer than a few minutes. She'd seen this before in other artists at The Copperfield House—most notably in Aurora, who'd stayed over the summer, writing music and painting. But Violet wasn't a typical "artist" type. She was Midwestern; she was a mother.

But that didn't mean she didn't need help.

"You'll let me know if you need anything," Julia said quietly as Greta's footsteps grew closer.

Violet spread her hands out on the table and stared at her fingers. "I just need a healthy grandson," she said quietly. "I'll do anything for him."

Greta bustled back into the kitchen, telling Julia what needed to be refilled, where to find new bottles of wine, and asking whether Julia thought they should put out ice cream just in case people wanted it. All the while, as Greta scuttled to and fro, Violet looked listless, hovering just left of a sunbeam that came in through the kitchen window. It was impossible to read her expression.

Just before Julia disappeared with a big vat of vanilla ice cream, she touched Violet's shoulder delicately and reminded her, "We want the same things. We want Adam to be healthy." But Violet couldn't look her in the eye.

As the party died down, Julia helped Anna to her

bedroom. Scarlet was hot on her heels with a fresh bottle of formula, which they'd prepared "just in case" Anna wasn't able to breastfeed tonight. Anna took one look at the formula and wrinkled her nose.

"Fed is best," Julia assured her.

Exhausted after her milk production continued to fail her, Anna set herself up on the bed, cradling Adam as she fed him his bottle. Her eyes were tender as she gazed down at him. Scarlet and Julia were wordless until Adam fell back asleep again, and Anna lay back on her bed pillows with Adam splayed across her chest. He looked impossibly small.

"Anna?" Julia asked, her tone low. "Did Dean ever mention anything about his mother?"

Anna's eyes flickered. "He sometimes said she was 'emotionally all over the place.' But he said it lovingly."

Julia palmed the back of her neck. How could she illustrate her worries without making Anna fully panic?

"I worry that Dean's death has had a huge impact on her," Julia offered. "That maybe we don't have the capabilities to help."

Anna bit her lip. "Me too."

"She better back off about this 'breast is best' business," Scarlet said, pacing the floor at the foot of the bed. "It's like she's forgotten what it means to be a brand-new mother."

"She'll get used to it," Julia tried.

"She's gone through so much," Anna said. Sleepiness transformed her face, and she settled deeper onto the pillow. "I can't thank you enough for trying to make her feel at home here. I just want her to know I still love Dean. And that she can be in the baby's life as much as she wants."

Ultimately, Anna's worries extended far beyond Violet now. She was a brand-new mother with a fresh set of problems—a future stretched out before her, riddled with fears and life lessons. Julia couldn't push it; she couldn't say anything that would keep Anna awake all night, heavy with discontent. She just had to hope Violet would calm down and settle into life with Adam. She had to hope her "warning" had been enough.

Chapter Ten

The private joys, frustrations, fears, and glories of those first few days of Adam's life would remain in Anna's heart forever. She found herself gazing endlessly at Adam's face, touching his tiny toes, stroking his thick hair, and wondering what was next for him. It seemed impossible that this tiny baby would one day grow up to be a man. Yet, as a new mother, that was all she could hope and pray for. That one day, he would fall in love, chase his dreams, and perhaps even move away—all in pursuit of building a life. "Your father wasn't allowed to do everything he dreamed of," Anna whispered. "It's up to you now."

Anna welcomed frequent visitors in her bedroom and the nursery—the Copperfields who couldn't get enough baby snuggles. The first day after the party, Scarlet hung around for hours, doting on baby Adam, changing his diaper, and giving him his bottle. Predictably, she also wanted to gossip about Smith. But Anna wasn't yet sure how to talk about him.

"I mean, he was with you?" Scarlet asked as she fed

Adam his bottle on day three of Adam's life. "He drove you to the hospital?"

Anna could do nothing but laugh. "Sure. We ran into each other that night. But it's not like it meant anything." This was the biggest lie she'd ever told.

"But he even came to a Copperfield family party to say hi to you," Scarlet protested. "The guy didn't speak to anyone for weeks. He flat-out refused to go to that party with me. And come on. We both have to acknowledge the way he looks at you!"

Anna arched her eyebrow, pretending not to understand. "Looks at me? Come on, Scarlet. I'm a new mother with a spare tire around my middle. I probably won't get enough beauty sleep to be seen outside the house in the foreseeable future."

Scarlet laughed. "I know you know what I'm talking about. You can't lie to me. I know you too well."

Anna's cheeks burned, and she crossed her legs beneath her on the mattress, watching as her baby suckled on the bottle. Just that morning, she'd strained and struggled to get him to latch to her breast. When he'd finally managed it, only a little milk had come out. She'd even connected her breasts to a horrific machine, a pump, to generate more milk production. Nothing seemed to be working.

"Smith's a weird guy," Scarlet observed, her eyes on Adam, "but he's also weirdly honest and true. I think it's because he's been through so much. When he shows up for you, it's because he really wants to."

"We don't really know him," Anna reminded Scarlet.

"True. But you know how you sometimes get feelings about people?" Scarlet asked.

Anna didn't nod or shake her head. Still, hearing her

sentiments about Smith echoed back from her cousin was strange. It anchored them.

But who was she kidding? This was no time to fall in love.

Of course, Violet stopped by the nursery frequently to see baby Adam. She brought several more baby items—equipment she'd recently read about that would "create a baby genius." Because Anna was so fatigued and over the moon, she didn't find it difficult to accept these gifts and call them "generous and kind." Perhaps in a week or two, they would outrage her again.

On the fifth day of Adam's life, Violet just happened to drop by the nursery when Anna's lactation consultant was leaving. Violet's eyes gleamed with happiness.

"I knew you'd listen to reason!" she cried as the lactation specialist disappeared down the hallway.

Violet seemed to take this as a sign to return to her previous-held status as "giver of parenting advice." Anna grimaced as Violet reminded her what had worked when Violet had been a new mother. "Always sleep when the baby sleeps," she said. "And they tell you not to let them cry it out, but many people say it only benefits them to let them calm themselves down. We all have to learn coping mechanisms at some point."

Anna's heartbeat quickened. "He's only five days old," she said, unable to resist.

"It's never too early to instill good habits," Violet said as she cradled Adam close.

It was often difficult to get Violet to leave Anna's room. She scrambled for more time with Adam, more conversation about Dean, and more parenting advice, so much so that it did Anna's head in. Once, she texted

Scarlet to save her, and Scarlet paraded down the hall, pretending to sob.

"He dumped me!" Scarlet cried as she entered the bedroom. "Oh gosh. I don't know what to do!" She then turned to blink knowingly at Violet, who raised her hands.

"Girls," Violet said, "you cannot take stock in men's opinions of you."

Realizing her tactic wasn't having the desired effect, Scarlet wailed louder and fell onto the bed. "Do you think I can talk to my cousin alone?" she whimpered.

When Violet finally got the hint, Scarlet's face transformed. "I have plenty more ideas where that came from."

"You're a lifesaver," Anna said.

Scarlet giggled and leaned against the wall beside the bed. "Look at him," she said, nodding toward Adam, tucked safely in Anna's arms. "I swear, he's already growing like a bean."

Anna allowed herself a moment of sorrow, realizing she'd already lost so much time with Adam.

Scarlet interrupted her reverie with a snap of her fingers. "You know who I saw downtown today?"

"Who?"

"Smith Watson," she said. "He was palling around with his dog, enjoying the winter sun and eating hot dogs. Then I saw him go into a flower shop and leave with a bouquet!"

Anna laughed. "You're a real spy. You know that, Scarlet?"

"It has to be for you," Scarlet said conspiratorially. "Who else would he buy flowers for?"

"Maybe he has a girlfriend on the island," Anna

suggested. "Or maybe she's coming to visit from the city?"

Even as she said it, that fiery jealousy returned, hovering over her heart. She couldn't control it.

"Yeah, right," Scarlet said. "Mark my words. You're the only person on his mind."

That evening after dinner, Anna returned to her bedroom to find a bouquet on the desk, along with a note that read:

Dear Anna and Adam,

I have never known anything as beautiful as helping you into the first era of your lives together. Thank you for giving me a window into the beauty of that world.

Yours,

Smith

Anna knew better than to daydream about romance. What had romance done for her, anyway? She'd fallen in love; she'd lost her love; she'd given birth to a fatherless baby. She'd revealed wretched truths about the world and about her place in it.

But as she drifted off to sleep that night, she couldn't help but dream of Smith's arms around her, of trading writing with Smith every night and helping each other become better, of drifting from one philosophical conversation to the next as Adam slept in his crib before them and a volatile Nantucket wind crashed into the house.

Maybe she was getting ahead of herself. But there was pleasure in that hope. It reminded her of what it meant to be alive.

Chapter Eleven

On the eighth day of Adam's life, Julia had a meeting with Smith set for eleven in the morning. She sat in her office with a mug of coffee and croissants, listening intently for Smith's footfalls on the staircase. If all had gone according to plan, Smith was set to bring her another twenty thousand words of his memoir today. She was mentally preparing herself to be disappointed in him, to urge him on.

There was a knock on the door.

"Come in!" Julia called.

Julia turned in her swivel chair just as Smith entered, wearing his traditional black with his hair tucked behind his ears. Luka followed him, his pink tongue lolling. Smith carried a large manila envelope, which he opened, retrieving what looked to be twenty thousand words printed out. Julia was flabbergasted.

"They're probably a mess," Smith said as Julia pored over the first few lines. "But it all came to me really easily."

As Smith sat beside her, Julia read the first few paragraphs. They were about a time in Smith's life that he hadn't discussed yet—when his mother had given birth to a stranger's baby, and Smith had been forced to make sure the baby was cared for. *"Obviously,"* Smith wrote, *"my mother wasn't willing to slow down, to give of herself, to show the baby an ounce of love. It made me understand what was lacking in my own infanthood. I could imagine myself screaming in a cradle as she burst back into the world, ready to take charge of her destiny again."*

As Julia read about Smith's half brother, tears welled in her eyes. She tried to blink them away, but many of them drifted to the pages below.

And within Smith's words, anger simmered. He hated his mother for abandoning his half brother, for forcing Smith to age up and become a sort of "father" at fifteen. *"The few friends I had at school couldn't comprehend the responsibilities I had at home,"* Smith wrote. *"And I watched my childhood shrivel up and die. Just like that."*

When Julia finished reading, she piled the pages back into a stack and turned to look at Smith. She knew, now, beyond a shadow of a doubt, that this kid had what it took in the writing world. He was immensely talented; his words and his spirit ran deep.

Anna could see that, too. Julia knew that even though Anna would never say it aloud. Anna had always been the same—a dark horse in a young, happy woman's body. She'd always listened to sad songs and gravitated toward heart-wrenching literature. Julia had always respected this, privately calling Anna an "old soul" to Jackson, who'd agreed.

"Has it affected you," Julia began, "being around Adam?"

What she meant was, had it reminded him too much

of being a father to his half brother? Had it made him miss home?

Smith raised his shoulders and traced his fingers through his hair. "Of course. But it's why the writing came out so smoothly. I miss him. So much." Smith's voice broke.

Julia's mouth went dry. Smith stared at the floor between their feet as though he'd revealed too much of himself and wasn't sure how to proceed.

Julia decided to stay professional. This way, she could prove how much she respected his work. "I have a few notes and ideas for edits," she said. "But I think we should proceed with the next section of the piece. If you feel ready?"

Smith nodded, and the corners of his lips turned up. He was proud, even as he unraveled his soul.

As Julia finished their meeting, there was another knock on the door. Without waiting for Julia's call, Greta propped open the door and peered in. Her eyes were fierce.

"Hey, Mom." Julia smiled and stood.

"I didn't mean to interrupt," Greta said, her eyes tracing Smith and Luka as they maneuvered through the office and disappeared into the shadowy hall.

"We're done," Julia said as she closed the door. Under her breath, she added, "He is so talented, Mom! His writing ripped my heart out."

Greta's eyes softened. She sat in the chair Smith had just vacated and crossed her hands over her lap. "Have you seen the way he looks at Anna?"

Julia wrinkled her nose and raised her shoulders. "And how do we feel about that?"

Greta tilted her head. "I'm pulling for them. Maybe

that's not right. I don't know." She sniffed. "But I came to tell you something."

Julia raised her eyebrows expectantly.

"I want to ask Violet to leave," Greta stated primly. "I've heard her nag Anna one too many times. And you should see her shoot daggers at Smith. Every time Smith comes to say hello to Violet, she mutters under her breath. Almost like she wants to put a spell on him."

Julia puffed out her cheeks. "We all want Violet to leave. But I'm worried."

"What about?"

"I don't know if she has anywhere to go," Julia said. She then explained that she and Anna asked when Larry Carpenter would visit. Violet had shown the whites of her eyes each time and assured them Larry would be there "any minute."

"But Larry is nowhere to be found," Julia affirmed. "And Anna hasn't heard from him."

Greta dropped back into her chair and rubbed her temples. Due to her elaborate array of night and day creams and addiction to sunblock, her seventy-year-old skin gleamed.

"If she tells me how to cook in my own kitchen one more time," Greta said, raising a finger, "I'll kick her out myself."

"Wow," Julia said with a laugh. "That woman is brave."

"Just stupid," Greta corrected her, making a face. "The nerve of some people!"

That afternoon, Julia padded to the second floor of the family half of The Copperfield House to cradle Adam, check on Anna, and search for Violet. It wasn't a surprise that Violet was seated at the edge of Anna's bed, spouting rhetoric about her own early days of motherhood.

And then, she delivered a piece of information that, finally, Julia could use.

"Of course, that was before I got my accounting license," she explained. "But I still worked here and there, especially after Dean got a bit older."

"What did you do for work?" Julia asked. Even as she said it, she thought I'd never cared about an answer more.

"I was a wedding planner," Violet said.

Immediately, Julia's and Anna's eyes locked. Inspiration flowed in the air between them. Finally, they could give Violet something to do.

"Violet!" Julia cried, her voice syrupy sweet. "You know I'm supposed to get married in three months?"

Violet's eyes widened. "I knew you were engaged. But in three months? That's quick!"

"You're telling me," Julia assured her. "I'm panicking. Charlie and I were hard at work planning the night Adam was born. And now, well. I don't even have my dress, let alone a venue."

Violet's eyes brimmed with light. For the first time in ages, she took her eyes off Adam and gazed intently at Julia. "You need help," she announced.

"You're telling me," Julia affirmed.

"Do you have time for something like that, Violet?" Anna asked meekly. "I know it's a lot."

Violet shot to her feet and latched her hands behind her back. "I'm going to need baseline information. Head count. Style. I still read wedding magazines religiously, so you don't need to worry about current styles. I know what's in and what's out."

Julia wanted to laugh at her sudden authoritative nature, but she managed to keep her giggles to herself.

"This is fantastic!" Julia cried. "I'm so underwater with my publishing clients. The wedding was going to be a rush job if it happened at all."

"Put your faith in me," Violet assured her. "Your wedding will be spectacular."

Chapter Twelve

Adam was ten days old and a miracle in every sense of the word. Anna wrapped her hand tenderly around his tiny foot and gazed at him while he was sleeping, wondering if she would ever have it in her to enter the "real" world again. A few writing clients had reached out to her in the past week, asking if she wanted to be featured in a travel magazine or travel up the coast for a gig. Anna no longer remembered how to chase her dreams. She'd given her heart to her baby. And it felt right.

With Adam fast asleep, Anna carried him downstairs to put the kettle on the stove and grab a snack. In the fridge was a selection of bottles from her as-yet inefficient pumping attempts, the milk glinting in the fridge light. She was closer to nursing properly than ever, but she still came up short.

As the kettle heated, Violet appeared in the kitchen with a thick selection of folders and her hair in a tight ponytail. Her face melted when she saw Adam in his carrier, and she knelt to touch his soft, little hand.

"What's all that?" Anna asked, nodding to the folders.

Violet grinned and sat down. "You won't believe this. Your mother hired me to plan her wedding!"

The kettle began to howl, and Anna turned and removed it.

"Maybe Dean never mentioned it. I used to plan weddings back when the kids were little," Violet explained. "I had a real knack for it, in fact. I got my start with my own wedding to Larry. Everyone said it was divine." Violet flipped through her phone to find a photograph of herself and Larry from their wedding—a time when Violet had been a slender and sweet-faced lady of twenty, and Larry had been the broad-shouldered captain of the football team. Anna's heart skipped a beat. Again, she wondered, where was Larry in all this? Why had he kept his distance?

Somewhere in the back of Anna's mind, she remembered something. Something about Dean's parents. Had Dean mentioned something about infidelity? About thinking his parents weren't right for each other? Anna and Dean had had hundreds of conversations in their nine months together. Probably ten percent of them had stuck.

"I have to make about a zillion phone calls today," Violet explained, tapping the folder. "Your mother gave me less than three months to plan the thing."

"She's an optimist," Anna said, filling a mug with tea.

"It's exhilarating," Violet said, her eyes on baby Adam. "I always thought showing my children I was a working woman was good. That women could do anything. That's why it's so good you're still writing. Adam will know you for the strong woman you are."

A shiver of annoyance went up and down Anna's spine. Everything Violet said seemed to have a layer of parental advice to it.

Before Anna could dwell, the door between the residency and the family house squealed open. Greta's voice filled the hallway. "It's not a problem at all. Right here. Look. We have too much of everything. You know how Bernard likes his pasta when he's upstairs writing!"

"Thank you, Mrs. Copperfield," Smith replied. "I can't believe I forgot to go to the store."

"I've told you over and over again," Greta said. "When you're at the residency, you're like a member of our family. What's ours is yours."

Smith appeared in the doorway before the pantry, assessing the wide selection of pasta, pasta sauces, and other canned goods. It was three in the afternoon, and Anna had to guess that Smith had spent the better part of the morning and afternoon writing and editing. She watched him as he reached for a box of penne and flipped it over to read the back. His hair was scraggly and wild, as though he'd played with it as he'd written, growing frustrated and flipping it around. A wave of passion flowed through her chest, one she wanted to immediately snuff out.

As though Smith could sense her, he flinched and turned around to catch her gaze. His smile was crooked yet immediate. He shook the pasta box as though it were a musical instrument.

"Hey," he said.

"Hey, back." Anna's voice wavered, and she sipped her tea, feeling approximately twelve years old.

From Smith's angle, he probably couldn't see Violet and vice versa. When he strode into the kitchen to speak to Anna more, he stalled, and his smile faltered. "Good afternoon," he said to Violet. Anna wasn't sure they'd ever spoken before.

"Hi there," Violet greeted, closing one of her folders. "Smith, right?"

"Yes, Mrs. Carpenter. I'm sorry that we haven't been properly introduced."

Smith tilted his head in a way indicating he knew all about Anna once being engaged, Dean's death, and Violet. It was wild to Anna that she could already read him so well—after hardly spending much time with him.

Anna wondered who he'd asked about her past. She could imagine Scarlet whispering the truth to him on the back porch as the waves rolled menacingly toward them and Smith looking intrigued. It didn't bother her, exactly, if this conversation had happened. It thrilled her to think that Smith had inquired about her when she wasn't around.

"I've heard you're a brilliant writer," Violet said.

"You heard all wrong," Smith assured her.

Violet chewed her lower lip. "You're just like my Dean," she said. "He was always so modest."

"I'm not modest, Mrs. Carpenter," Smith said. "I'm just honest."

Violet's face fell, and she stared down at the folders before her as though they could offer her some explanation.

Smith shook the box of pasta again and shifted his eyes toward Anna. Anna's heart dropped into her stomach. The intensity in the air between them made every hair on her body stand on end.

Was it true what Violet said? Was Smith anything

like Dean? They didn't look similar, that was for sure. And their personalities seemed worlds apart.

But Violet was seeing what she wanted to see.

"I'd better get back," Smith said, stepping toward the hall. As he twisted around, he paused, gazed down at the floor, and then dropped to retrieve a small piece of paper. "I think you dropped this, Anna." He swished it through the air and placed it delicately on Anna's palm.

Anna's heart thudded. On the paper was a phone number. She closed her hand around it as though it were a precious thing. And when she glanced back up, Smith was gone.

In his carrier, Adam wailed and kicked his feet. Already, Violet fled the kitchen table to retrieve a bottle of breast milk and feed him. Anna's heart pounded so loud that she could hardly hear the baby's cries.

* * *

Hours later, long after the rest of The Copperfield House was asleep and Adam had long since closed his eyes, Anna retrieved the slip of paper from the inside of her book, placed it on the center of her desk, and considered what to do.

If she chickened out, Smith would take that as a sign she didn't like him. He would move on, and she would continue her course of new motherhood. That would be that. But the idea that Smith wouldn't look at her like she'd hung the moon and the stars—made her heart sink.

If she did text Smith, what then? It was risky, especially with Violet in The Copperfield House. Maybe she could contact him and tell him she wanted to be friends for the time being. She could explain everything.

Then again, wasn't she being sort of presumptuous, thinking that Smith wanted anything romantic? Maybe he just wanted to be friends. More than that, maybe the slip of paper didn't have his number on it at all!

Anna chuckled to herself, imagining texting some random person—the real owner of the phone number. Maybe it was one of James's high school friends. Maybe it was someone Laura had met in college.

Thinking "what the heck," Anna typed in the number and wrote:

> Hey. It's Anna.

Almost immediately, the number read it and responded.

> Meet on the back porch? I'll grab two beers.

Anna thought she was going to fall to her knees with fear. With shaky hands, she did her makeup, checked and re-checked herself in the mirror, ensured Adam was warm enough, then raised his carrier from the ground to heave it downstairs. She would have to get used to bringing the baby everywhere she went. She was his home.

Smith was seated on the enclosed porch with two bottles of beer on the table before him. He hadn't turned on the light, and the moon's reflection glowed over them, giving him a dark profile. Anna's mouth was dry with fear. Wordlessly, Smith uncapped her beer and handed it over to her, then clinked his with hers.

This was Anna's first beer since she'd found out she was pregnant. It was smooth and nutty and refreshing, and she drank too much of it in a single gulp. When she placed the beer back on the table, she followed Smith's gaze to Adam, who remained asleep.

"I hope you don't mind that I brought him."

Smith's eyes caught the light of the moon. "Why would I mind?"

Anna's heart was warm. She took another sip of beer and smiled.

"I wasn't sure you were going to text me," Smith said.

"I wasn't sure if I was going to either."

Smith laughed gently. In the silence that followed, Anna's brain whirred. What was she supposed to say? Was she here to flirt with him? She should have thought this through.

"You know," Smith said, turning to watch the waves roll up along the beach, "I've enjoyed being here a lot more than I thought I would."

"Me too," Anna said.

Smith arched his eyebrow. "This wasn't always home for you." He said it as though he already knew.

Anna took another swig of beer. She tried not to remember Dean's face, how he'd gazed at her on the other side of the table and asked her to be his wife.

"It's new," Anna explained. "But I fell in love with it quickly. And now, it's Adam's first home. I think we're here to stay."

"Home. What a concept." Smith said it without sounding irritated. Rather, he seemed mystified. He bowed his head toward the corner, where Anna now saw Luka was fast asleep, his belly stretched out.

Anna smiled. She loved how much Smith loved his dog.

"So. How is it?" Smith asked, bowing his head toward Adam.

"Oh." Anna furrowed her brow. She recognized that Smith didn't want a boxed answer, like so many other people. Ordinarily, she was supposed to say, "It's the most magical experience of my life" or "It's so rewarding!"

But instead, she said, "It's true that I've never known a love like this. But it's also true that I've never felt like more of a failure."

Smith eyed her warily.

"Maybe it's embarrassing to explain."

"Nothing embarrasses me," Smith said. Anna believed him.

"I really wanted to breastfeed him," Anna offered. There was a jump in her voice. "But he finds it difficult to latch on, and my milk production is down. I pump and pump and pump, and it's never enough." Anna closed her eyes. She'd never said any of this aloud. "Dean's mom won't stop pestering me about it either. It's like she's always right there, reminding me that I'm not treating her son's baby well enough."

"Dean?"

"My fiancé," Anna said, her eyes still closed. "He died."

Smith gave no indication of whether he knew this or not.

"Anna," Smith began instead. "Your body has already been through one of the most traumatic events in your lifetime."

Anna frowned as he leaned across the table.

"You brought a baby into the world," Smith continued. "You were in so much pain. You need to have compassion for your body. You need to remember what it's done for you."

Anna blinked back tears. She'd never anticipated this.

She took a big swig of beer and touched her lower belly, which remained deflated and strange after the birth of Adam. She'd often wondered, selfishly, if her body would ever return to its pre-pregnancy form.

And now, Smith was telling her not to demand that of her body.

"Listen," Smith began, "I hate to make this about me. But just as an example, there was this one time that I was in a major car accident. I broke both of my legs."

Anna flinched. "My goodness."

Smith waved his hands. "I was so frustrated with myself. I couldn't walk. I could hardly get around at all. And I'd hurt my wrist, too, which meant it was difficult to operate the crutches. I was totally lost. And then, the minute I had a bit more strength in my legs and arm, I pushed myself too hard and, you guessed it, broke something again."

"No!"

Smith nodded and crossed his arms. Anna wondered if this story would go in his memoir. More than that, she wondered if he was telling the full truth. Had it really been a car accident? Had his mother been drunk and crashed with him inside?

"I had to have patience," Smith said. "It was a tough lesson to learn. But I'm so grateful I did. Around that time, I forced myself to sit down and write about what was happening. And, obviously, that changed my life." Smith gestured back toward The Copperfield House as though its mighty structure was proof enough of how far he'd come.

Before Anna could think of something else to say, Adam opened his tiny red mouth and wailed. Anna burst to her feet to tend to him. But just like that afternoon, someone else beat her to it. In a flash, Smith had the baby in his arms. He cradled Adam as though he'd cradled hundreds of babies, as though he'd helped them drift off to sleep, as though he knew exactly what was on their minds.

"Wow," Anna breathed as Adam's cries quieted. "Are you a baby whisperer?"

Smith laughed, but the look in his eyes gave her pause. There was tremendous pain there. Had Smith had a baby with someone? Had tragedy struck?

Anna couldn't stop herself from asking, "There's so much I still don't know about you. But I have the feeling you know so much about me."

With Adam fast asleep again, Smith bent to place him gently in his carrier. Remaining in a squat, he peered up at her, unsmiling. "I don't know anything about you, Anna. But I'd like to. If you'll let me."

Anna bit her lower lip as her heart pounded. This felt more intimate than kissing.

"How do you know so much about babies?" Anna asked.

Smith's face drooped, and he got to his feet, stretching out his arm to fetch his empty beer. "That's a story for another time," he said softly. He then pressed the screen door open and gazed back at her. Because of the moonlight, his skin looked silver. "Maybe we can do this again?"

Anna nodded. "I'd like that."

And with that, Smith was gone.

Chapter Thirteen

Ella and Will's band was featured at an iconic music venue in the Lower East Side in mid-February. Most of the Copperfield clan planned a spontaneous trip to the city to see them perform, packing up their suitcases, making dinner reservations, and speaking in circles about what touristy things to do. Because Adam was less than a full month old, Anna told Julia that she knew she was out. Julia's heart felt bruised. She promised her daughter she would remain behind, too. But Anna begged her to go. "You've been working so hard," she said. "Take Charlie and go to the city. You deserve it."

A few days before the big trip to Manhattan, Julia met with Smith in her office to review another selection of pages. Like usual, Luka slept at Smith's feet as Smith discussed his reasoning for specific scenes—why he showed his mother as "kind" in one scene, only to have her kindness drop out in the next. Julia had come to learn that Smith had upward of ten official and unofficial stepfathers, most of whom had been tremendously cruel.

Smith also waffled with how to portray his half brother and explained that he wanted to protect his brother's identity at all costs.

When they finished the meeting, Julia asked Smith why he wasn't going to Manhattan with the rest of the Copperfields and the other artists. "You lived in the city for years before you came to The Copperfield House," she said. "Don't you miss it?"

"I don't miss it at all," Smith confessed with a wry laugh. "I know that sounds strange. But so many things changed in my childhood all the time. I could never count on anything to stay the same. I think I untrained the muscle in your brain that allows you to miss something."

Julia burned to ask him if Smith would miss Anna after he left The Copperfield House. Everyone knew they were thick as thieves. Yet every time Julia brought this up with Anna, Anna maintained they were "just friends."

It was difficult to read Violet's take on the matter. That afternoon, Julia met Violet in the kitchen to go over Violet's recent work on the wedding and catch up. Now that Anna's breast milk had come in and she was nursing full-time, Violet had backed off on giving unsolicited parenting advice. This was a relief for everyone. Plus, she was too distracted with Julia's wedding to notice fully when Anna did something that wasn't completely "Violet-approved." This was yet another blessing.

Somehow, they'd fallen into a rhythm with one another. Yet Julia was always watching, waiting for it to fall apart again. The foundation was rocky.

Alana entered the kitchen to grab a diet soda. "More wedding planning?" she asked as she popped open the can.

"It's never complete till the day after," Violet assured her.

"You might have to plan mine!" Alana said. "Jeremy has all these dreams for it. But my first wedding was so iconic. It's difficult for me not to compare." She sighed and gazed through space thoughtfully, remembering her long-lost time of grandeur. Although Julia knew she was very happy with Jeremy, Alana always found reasons to bring up her past.

"I think we can make it just as iconic," Violet said, scribbling something down on her notepad. Julia had long since given up on reading her handwriting.

"There they are again," Alana said, bowing her head toward the window. "I swear, they're always going up and down, up and down."

Out along the sand were Anna, Smith, and Luka. Anna had baby Adam wrapped across her chest, bundled tightly against the wind. Her face was open with laughter as Smith told a story, articulating everything with his hands. It was impossible to guess what Smith spoke of. It certainly had nothing to do with what he'd written so far in his memoir.

Violet raised her head and clicked her pen. She looked captivated by them, her eyes glossy. For a moment, Julia was terrified she would burst into tears. In another reality, the man walking across the sand with Adam and Anna was Dean rather than Smith.

After a dramatic pause, Violet said, "You know, when Dean was a toddler, he couldn't get enough carrots? He was obsessed with them. And, silly parents that we were, we handed them over. They were vitamins, right? Well. It didn't take long till he turned orange!"

As Violet told this story, her eyes traced Smith and Anna, almost as though she was thinking Smith was Dean. But that was impossible, Julia told herself. Violet was a bit strange, but she wasn't crazy.

Julia swallowed the lump in her throat. "Hey, Violet?"

Violet slowly dragged her gaze back toward Julia and blinked at her.

"Come to New York with us," Julia offered.

"Oh my! Yes," Alana cried. "You totally have to." There was a false ring to her voice that only Julia, being her sister, could hear.

Violet furrowed her brow. "I don't know. I have all this work to do for the wedding. And Anna needs me to help with Adam."

"Anna is doing just fine," Julia said. "My mother doesn't want to go into the city either, so she'll be here to help."

Violet rubbed the back of her neck. "I've never been to the city."

Alana clapped her hands. "This is your chance, Violet. It's the closest you'll ever get! When you go back to Ohio, you'll regret not going."

* * *

Three days later, Julia, Violet, Alana, Jeremy, Charlie, and Bernard piled into Julia's SUV, armed with a picnic basket ladened with Greta's sandwiches, salads, and chocolate chip cookies with sea salt. As Julia backed out of the driveway, Greta and Anna waved from the front porch, wishing them well. Julia braced herself for Violet to back out, insisting on staying behind to care for Adam. But Violet remained quiet. When Julia glanced at her reflection in the rearview mirror, she saw a woman with the expectant and hopeful eyes of a young girl.

Of course, if Violet knew what Anna and Julia had discussed that morning, she wouldn't have been happy. As Anna had wrapped Adam to her chest, securing his sleeping body, Julia had said, "I think it's time to contact Larry Carpenter and see what's up."

Anna had said, "I've been thinking the same thing."

They were both sure now that Violet wasn't telling the truth. That she'd "moved" to Nantucket without explaining why.

Anna still had Dean's cell phone. She'd pocketed it the day of the accident and never offered it to anyone— not the authorities, not Dean's family. "I'll find his dad's phone number," she'd said. Apparently, she still kept the phone charged, perhaps as a last attempt to cling to Dean. This detail broke Julia's heart.

On the drive, the Copperfields were boisterous. Bernard had a million ideas for topics of conversation, and he demanded they dig into philosophy, language, mathematics, and stories in a way that made Julia's head spin. "Dad," Alana protested, "not all of us are known geniuses, okay? Mom isn't even here!"

Twice, Bernard made Violet laugh—real, belly laughs, and the sound warmed Julia's heart. Maybe they could save this woman with enough laughter, conversation, and good food. Julia only wished she could be honest about needing help.

Hours later, Julia parked the SUV in a parking garage in the Lower East Side. Others in the Copperfield family were already in the city and would meet them at the venue later. Scarlet and Quentin were meeting with producers; Catherine had come early to see a friend. Charlie sidled up with Julia and laced his fingers through hers, his eyes glinting. Julia knew he was thinking about when they'd moved to the city without a plan, back when they'd been reckless and first in love. She was thinking about it, too.

Before the concert, they ate at a Chinese restaurant with a Michelin star. Violet's eyes were enormous as she read the menu, trying to make sense of fare she'd never heard of before. Adorably, she ordered a white wine with a meek voice and tried to laugh at herself. "I'm such a small-town girl at heart," she stammered.

Ultimately, Julia and Alana decided to order most of the menu so everyone at the table could taste a bit of everything. There was Peking duck, mapo tofu, hot pot, sweet and sour pork, and wonton soup, along with plenty of appetizers wrapped in fried dough. Julia watched as Violet took her first bite of Peking duck and closed her eyes at the intensity of the flavors. When she opened them again, they remained slits.

"My goodness," she whispered.

"Not bad, huh?" Alana asked with a laugh.

Violet swallowed another bite. "Dean always accused me of being unadventurous," she said after a pause. "He always urged me to try new things."

Julia felt momentarily deflated. She worried that mentioning Dean would drag Violet back into the depths again. But instead, Violet dug into the mapo tofu and took a large sip of wine, her eyes dancing to Bernard, who was ready with yet another story. Julia's heart swelled. She texted Anna back in Nantucket to report.

JULIA: All good here.

JULIA: Violet seems to be coming into her own.

JULIA: How is it going there?

Chapter Fourteen

Anna held Dean's cell phone with both hands. It glinted up at her; it displayed a photograph of Dean and Anna during their sixth-month anniversary dinner in downtown Seattle. The smile on Anna's face was difficult to see. Her happiness and carefree nature made her look like a completely different person. When Anna peered at her reflection in the mirror, she saw a haggard young mother who hadn't gotten enough sleep.

Smith urged her not to think of herself that way. "Words have power over us," he'd said. "You have to think of yourself in the positive."

Anna no longer remembered how she knew Dean's phone's passcode. Had he told it to her? Had they really had that kind of laissez-faire relationship? Anna typed it in and was immediately drawn into Dean's world prior to his death. He'd even taken several photographs on the hike that had killed him—Anna in her raincoat next to an enormous pine tree and a selfie of them both with a mountain hovering behind them. Several photos back were the engagement ring, seemingly before Dean had given it to Anna. Maybe he'd sent it to a friend for approval. Maybe he'd sent it to his mother.

Anna had never gotten up the nerve to read Dean's text messages. It felt like crossing a boundary. There had assuredly been stuff Dean hadn't told her about. That was the nature of a nine-month relationship.

Anna found Dean's father's phone number easily. It had Dean's Ohio area code. Anna took a deep breath as she typed the numbers into her own phone. For some reason, she was terrified.

The phone rang and rang. Anna considered hanging up and sending an explanation via text. People usually didn't answer the phone if they didn't know who it was.

And then, abruptly, a familiar voice said, "Hello? This is Larry."

Anna's mouth went dry. Little Adam slept on in his carrier, his fingers curled loosely, his black hair in ringlets around his ears.

"Larry. Mr. Carpenter. Hi." Anna swallowed. "It's Anna. Anna Crawford?"

Larry's voice lightened. "Anna. It's so good to hear from you."

Anna loosened her shoulders. This was just Dean's father, a man who'd always been kind to her. A man who'd loved his son and lost him.

"I guess, um. I wanted to reach out. And tell you more about your grandson? If you want to hear?"

Larry's voice became just a crackle. "Yes. I mean. Of course." He sighed. "I figured you'd had him by now. I wanted to reach out. I don't have any excuse."

Anna's heart pumped. This confirmed one thing: Violet and Larry weren't in contact.

"Tell me," Larry begged. "What's his name?"

"His name is Adam." Anna's throat swelled. "He's gorgeous, with a full head of black hair and Dean's eyes. He was born almost a month ago."

Larry sounded like he was crying. Anna closed her eyes, but a single tear escaped and traced its way to her chin. Death seemed like an impossible darkness. They were all carrying Dean's in their own, messy way.

"Will you send me a photograph?" Larry finally managed.

"Of course," Anna whispered. "I'll send you as many as you like."

Larry gasped and laughed into the phone. "I'm sorry. I'm all over the place."

"I don't blame you at all. This is a lot to hear." Anna rubbed her temple and urged herself to be brave, to ask what she'd called about. "And you know, of course, that Violet is here?"

"Oh. Is she?" Larry's voice narrowed to a string, proof of his guilt. "No, I didn't know. Last I heard, she was staying out in the apartments by the mall. I hadn't checked in on her recently." He sniffed. "I meant to. I meant to do a lot of things."

Anna's chest ached. She imagined Violet alone in a shoddy apartment by the mall—rising in the morning and going to bed at night as her husband carried on without her.

"Do you mind if I ask"—Anna hesitated—"what happened?"

Larry sighed again. "We separated shortly after Dean passed away. I couldn't pretend to be happy in that marriage anymore, and I assumed she felt the same way. Anyway, she packed up her things and left. We signed the divorce papers in autumn. But we didn't even have to see each other to end the marriage officially. Isn't that wild? That you can have an entire life with someone and finalize its ending through an anonymous lawyer with halitosis?"

Outrage and pity formed a storm in Anna's heart. Larry's words, *"I couldn't pretend to be happy in that marriage anymore,"* swirled in her mind. Hadn't he considered Violet's feelings once?

Dean would have been wild with anger. He would have demanded more of his parents. He'd had a brilliant moral compass. He'd loved harder than most.

"I'm with someone else now," Larry explained. "We're selling the house and moving to Florida."

"Oh. Florida." Anna's voice was limp. She fought her urge to hang up the phone.

"Maybe we can visit you and Adam sometime this summer," Larry suggested. "Although, if you say he has Dean's eyes, I don't know if I can take it. The memories are still painful."

* * *

After Anna got off the phone with Larry, she wrapped Adam to her chest and wandered through The Copperfield House like a ghost. With most everyone gone, the only sound she heard was Greta typing away in her office. When she passed through the door between the residency and the family house, she discovered the kitchen echoing, the halls filled with shadows. A knock on Smith's door revealed nothing.

Anna walked tentatively downstairs with her hand wrapped around Adam's head. Ever since the night on the back porch with Smith, when they'd shared beers, she and Smith had hardly gone a day without seeing one another. His "baby whisperer" status in her life had only elevated. He'd even taught her a trick or two to handle Adam's gas, his anxious cries, and his fatigue. Only once had he hinted why he knew all this. Something about a "brother." Something about "the only person who'd ever really loved him."

Despite the tension between them, their conversations, and similar wavelengths, Anna was still not sure how to categorize their relationship. Scarlet insisted it was romantic, and Anna insisted it was bigger than that. "You need to kiss him already," Scarlet teased. "Get it over with." But Anna was frightened that kissing would ruin the beautiful understanding between them. She didn't want to scare him away.

"I don't know if I'll ever manage to have normal relationships with people," Smith had said more than once, alluding to his horrific past. "I might be too damaged."

Anna had decided to take this as a warning sign. Smith didn't want anything with her. And that had to be okay.

Just before Anna slipped back into the family half of the house, she heard the door open and scream shut. A dog huffed through the house, appearing around the corner and smiling up at her.

"Luka!" she said as he galloped closer.

Smith appeared in the hallway immediately after. His cheeks were ruddy, and he tugged his winter hat from his head to reveal sloppy black curls. In his left hand, he carried a large bouquet—roses and lilies and baby's breath. Anna's heart seized.

"What are those?" Anna asked.

"What do they look like?" Smith teased. He stopped a few feet away from Anna and twirled the bouquet in his hands. "Don't you read the calendar?"

Anna's heart pounded. Due to the nature of giving birth and caring for a brand-new baby, she found it difficult to keep track of dates and times. It was as though she floated through time and space.

And then, it hit her. "Is it Valentine's Day?"

Smith smiled, and his dimples deepened. He passed the bouquet foolishly, wearing an expression that was difficult to read. If Anna had to guess, she'd say he'd never bought anyone flowers before. Her cheeks burned with the intensity of his eyes.

"They're beautiful," Anna whispered.

If only Scarlet was here to see this, Anna thought. She would have a field day.

It was evening, which called for beers on the back porch. Smith set up The Copperfield House's brand-new Bluetooth speaker and attached it to his shoddy phone to play one of Anna's favorite songs, "Linger" by The Cranberries. Anna sang gently, wondering what Adam thought of the vibrations through her chest. When it was over, she selected "There Is A Light That Never Goes Out."

"The Smiths?" Smith cackled and threw his head back.

Anna nodded and matched his smile. "Were you named after them?"

"Gosh, I hope not," Smith joked.

"Come on," Anna shot back. "This song is amazing."

They sat in silence for a moment, listening to the jangle of a forty-year-old British pop song with heavy depressive undertones. A roommate from college had first shown Anna The Smiths, calling them "essential listening for the college era." Smith, of course, had never gone to college. But she liked this about him—the fact that every step of the way, he'd had a different experience from her. It made his writing strange and exciting. It made their conversations deviate wildly.

When the song was over, Anna turned down the volume. "I just made that phone call I was telling you about."

Smith's ears perked up. "To Larry?"

"Yes." Anna winced. "He didn't know anything about Adam. He's thinking about moving to Florida with his new girlfriend."

"Oh, no." Smith shook his head sadly and stared at the bouquet, which they'd placed in a vase in the center of the porch table.

"I just keep thinking about what Violet was like when she first got here," Anna continued. "She pretended she'd be here for just a couple of weeks, even as she dragged four suitcases up the staircase. And she waded her way out of every conversation about anything real. She's been hiding."

Smith closed his eyes. Sensing something wrong, Luka rushed him and placed his nose on Smith's thigh. "We lie to cope with the things we can't handle," Smith said finally.

Anna bit her lip. "I wish I could tell her it's okay to tell the truth. That we'll accept her. That we'll help her."

"She's not the kind of woman who accepts help," Smith went on delicately.

Anna knew he was right. But she still wasn't prepared for what he told her next.

"Sometimes she cooks for me," Smith said. "She comes up to my bedroom with big bowls of pasta with homemade sauce and parmesan. There's this look in her eyes like it's really important that she take care of me. Like she has to save everyone but herself."

Smith's voice broke. Slowly, he raised his chin, and the moonlight that swam through the night sky reflected off his glossy eyes. "She doesn't know how it kills me," he went on slowly. "My mother never cooked for me like that. And it's like, I'm seeing into how so many other people grew up. How much love they felt from their parents. Sometimes thinking about it rips me up so much that I can't write for the rest of the day. I can just eat the beautiful pasta and stare into space."

Chapter Fifteen

Ella and Will's band was in the midst of their second encore of the night when Anna's text came in. Distracted, Julia tugged her phone from her pocket and read it.

ANNA: Larry and Violet are divorced. Larry has moved on. Didn't even know Adam was born.

Julia shoved the phone back into her pocket and gave Violet a sidelong glance. Effervescent and alive after a few too many glasses of wine, Violet had both hands in the air and swayed to the music, her hips churning. Although she'd never heard this song before, she tried to sing along with the chorus, matching the rest of the voices in the venue. Julia's heart went out to her. Violet had been alone for months—and she'd been too terrified to say so.

After the final song cut out and the lights flashed on above them, Violet strung her arm around Julia's and cried, "This was one of the best nights of my life!"

Julia smiled. "It isn't over yet, honey."

In the wake of the concert, Bernard led them, whistling, down the block to a local bar with five-dollar draft pints and overfilled glasses of wine. During their stint in Manhattan last year, Julia and Bernard had frequented the place during Bernard's book tour. The bartender welcomed Bernard back with a clap on the shoulder. "I read that book of yours," he said. "It took me six months. It was the only book I read all year. But I loved it!" Bernard laughed heartily and dropped his head back.

Violet, Charlie, Jeremy, Alana, and Julia snuggled into a booth with beers and wine. Violet's eyes were enormous as she took in the vibrant bar, the young people flirting and chatting, the chandelier glinting from the ceiling.

"We don't have nights like this in Ohio," Violet said wistfully.

Charlie snapped his fingers. "I've been meaning to ask you more about Dayton," he said. "What's it like there?"

Violet raised her shoulders. "For a long time, I thought it was the only home I'd ever know."

"And now?" Alana asked.

Violet knocked back half of her beer in one gulp and smiled dreamily. Julia wasn't sure she'd heard the question. She twirled her wedding band around her finger and continued looking around the bar. As Jeremy brought up Ella and Will's "new sound," a stranger in his fifties approached with a James Bond swagger. He sidled up next to Violet and said, "Can I get you another beer?"

Violet's eyes were illuminated with surprise. She looked like a teenager who'd just been embarrassed in front of her friends at school. "Oh. I don't know," she stuttered, staring into her beer.

"She's married," Alana said after a strange moment of silence.

The fifty-something man raised his hands and laughed. "I should have known. But you can't fault a man for trying, can you? Have a good night."

Violet giggled sadly to herself and sipped her beer. Alana and Julia locked eyes over the table. Julia wagged her eyebrows, trying to tell Alana wordlessly that Violet was, in fact, single. That their suspicions had been correct. But Alana just furrowed her brow and mouthed, "What?"

"If only Larry could see this," Violet said softly, her glass of beer raised. "He always wanted me to be someone like this. A woman of the world." She closed her eyes, and her shoulders shook. It was difficult to tell if she was laughing or crying. "You know, he begged me to move to a bigger city after we had Dean. He was so sure we'd be happier. That we'd be giving Dean more opportunities. But I was terrified he would meet someone else in the city. I was scared he'd leave me." Violet opened her eyes again, and they were blotchy and red. "Isn't that funny?"

Julia wasn't sure what was funny about that. It seemed as though Violet was having an out-loud conversation with herself, falling through amorphous memories that were gradually turning into swords.

"You're here now, babe," Alana recited, clinking her glass with Violet's. "And you know what? They don't tell women in their forties this. But you can do whatever you want."

Violet's smile faded, and she looked at Alana as though she'd never seen her before.

"Seriously," Alana went on. "Look at me? I completely changed my life a few years ago, and I wouldn't change a thing. I was absolutely miserable. For years! And now, Jeremy and I have really built something." Alana wrapped her hand around Jeremy's bicep as Jeremy smiled adoringly.

"We all changed our lives," Julia reminded Violet.

"Nothing will ever remain the same," Alana continued. "And it's best if you take the reins."

Violet looked thoughtful, tilting her head. The speakers blared eighties dance music from Julia's childhood. It gave her funny images of Greta dancing in the kitchen with a wooden spoon.

And then, she said, "I think we should go dancing. Who's with me?"

Violet raised her hands in the air and cried out, "Me!"

"I guess we'd better follow her lead," Alana quipped. "But I have to get on her level. Who's up for a shot?"

* * *

The next day, Julia drove back to Nantucket with a thunderous headache—one for the record books. It put some of her hangovers in college to shame. In the back seat, the other Copperfields, Charlie, Jeremy, and Violet were quiet. Julia suspected they were all trying not to throw up.

Violet pulled her suitcase from the trunk and made her way inside. Julia followed her upstairs, where she disappeared into her own bedroom. She suspected she wouldn't pester Anna all afternoon and into the evening.

She'd had one of the biggest nights of her life. And now, she was paying for it.

When Julia reached her bedroom, she received a ping on her phone. It was a reminder she'd written herself a week ago: Meeting with Smith at 5 p.m. That was in half an hour. She cursed herself and padded downstairs to make a pot of coffee. She should have had the foresight to cancel.

Smith arrived just on time. He slipped the folder of his newly written pages onto the desk, sat in the chair beside her, and placed his hand on Luka's head. Luka wagged his tail and peered up at Julia hopefully, as though he'd contributed to Smith's pages and just wanted her assurance that they were good.

Smith and Julia weren't bothered by small talk. Julia dove into the pages immediately, reading about how Smith's mother had once been in the midst of a bipolar attack and had "accidentally or on purpose, it was unclear," burned him with a hot skillet. The story made her blood run cold. When she finished, she blinked up at him and set the stack of pages back on the desk.

"Smith," she breathed. "I just want to say. I'm so sorry that happened to you."

Smith waved his hand. "I've dealt with it."

Julia wasn't sure how anyone could conceivably deal with something like that.

Julia swallowed. "We're nearing the end of the book. I can hardly believe it."

Smith remained quiet.

"I'm curious," she went on, "about the ending. How do you finish things with your mother?"

Smith rubbed his neck and looked out the window.

Julia followed his gaze to find a cardinal on a nearby tree branch, whose dark eyes seemed to peg them.

"I mean," Julia continued, "where is your mother now?"

Smith seemed unwilling to answer such a forward question. He swallowed, his eyes still on the cardinal.

"I've been thinking," he said, "about this book tour you mentioned."

"What about it?"

"I'm just wondering how honest I need to be," Smith inquired. "How much of myself do I need to give the readers during the Q&A sessions?"

"Generally, books sell better when the readers think they're getting something special and unique from you," Julia said.

Smith looked deflated. Julia suddenly hated that Smith's pain was his commodity. It was hers, too. But that was the nature of the business, wasn't it? This was something she'd had to accept long ago.

After a long pause, Smith spoke.

"I see. Well." He coughed. "I have an idea about how to end the book. I don't know if I feel up to talking about it, but I'll have the pages for you soon. Okay?"

Julia's head rang like a bell. She thanked Smith and ushered him out of her office, grateful to be alone again. But no sooner had she sat down than she received a text from her father, asking for her presence in his upstairs office. It had been ages since Bernard had let Julia into his writing world—and Julia wasn't inclined to say no. No matter how exhausted she was.

Julia hurried upstairs to find Bernard at his desk with a partial stack of a manuscript before him. His grizzled hair was wild and untamed around his ears, and his cheeks were bright red after his evening of drinking at the bar. Unlike the others, he hadn't gone dancing and had, instead, held court with a collection of writers who were getting their MFA at City College. This had culminated in his inviting all of them to The Copperfield House to write in the residency.

"I wanted to let you know," Bernard said, "that I'm nearly finished with the next manuscript. I could foresee a publishing date in autumn. We can hit the all-famous Christmas shopping traffic again." He smiled knowingly. He often teased her about publishing "sales" and how unimportant they were to the artist when compared to the publisher.

"Wow. Dad. That's amazing." Julia crossed her legs beneath her and bent to read the first few lines of the new manuscript. They had Bernard's traditional voice along with a newfound sense of humor. His most recent book, a work of autofiction set in a prison, hadn't had space for jokes. It would be a fresh twist.

"Your mother has refused to let me read her recent manuscript," Bernard stated. "I'm hoping we can make a trade."

Julia laughed. Her mother was far more stubborn than her father when it came to showing her work. You practically had to pry it out of her hands before she felt it was "completely perfect."

After a brief discussion about Bernard's work, Julia found herself shifting gears and discussing her working relationship with Smith. It wasn't often that she came to her father for advice, but this called for it.

Julia explained the dynamics of Smith's memoir, about all he'd been through, and about how unwilling he was to share specific details about his mother and his half brother.

"I'm getting the sense that he has cold feet," Julia said.

Bernard dragged his fingers through his beard ponderously. "He's twenty-six?"

Julia nodded.

"He's on the brink of discovering something," Bernard said.

"What's that?"

Bernard sighed. "That you don't owe anyone your soul. That giving away too much of yourself negates your own power. It's something all writers struggle with. But it sounds like Smith is wise beyond his years."

Julia's voice wavered. "He's been through a lot. But like I said. He's signed a contract. We sent him a hefty advance. And more than that, we brought him here, to The Copperfield House, to finish his memoir. I have so much riding on this book. And the publishing house is counting on it to round out the sales this year."

Bernard remained quiet, and Julia stewed with shame. Here it was again: the topic of money.

"I just hope he knows what he's getting into," Bernard said.

Julia's hangover had wandered through her head and into her neck, where her tendons were taut. They seemed apt to snap.

"Oh," Julia said as an afterthought. "Anna found out Violet is divorced. She doesn't have a home to go back to. Can you believe that?"

Bernard's eyes were cloudy and difficult to read. He rubbed his beard and muttered, "Fascinating."

"What do you mean?"

"Violet is demonstrating what Smith is learning in real time," he said. "She understands there's a currency in secrets, in rewriting your past the way you want to."

"But she's been lying to us," Julia pointed out.

"We all pick the details we want to share," Bernard reminded her. "We're all writers, in a sense. Unfortunately for Violet, she couldn't fully hide from the past. But maybe we can help her write a better future."

Chapter Sixteen

The shift in Violet after the trip to Manhattan happened gradually and then all at once, similar to a flower opening its petals in the light of spring. She smiled more and demanded of Anna less. She offered to help with Adam rather than take over responsibilities completely, thinking she knew best, and she frequently joined the Copperfield women on the back porch for wine and snacks, listening just as much as she gossiped. She was day to December Violet's night. Anna found herself genuinely adoring her company and questioning why she'd ever wanted her to go back to Ohio in the first place. She was a dream.

At the beginning of March, as early spring light spilled through the kitchen window, Anna asked Julia why, in her opinion, Violet had come out of her shell. "You didn't talk to her about Larry, did you?"

Julia was chopping garlic on the counter. "Nothing like that. But Alana and I gave her a pep talk about making different choices in your forties. About building a new life. Maybe she took it to heart?"

It seemed too simple to Anna. She shared the information with Smith, who agreed with her. "People don't make shifts that quickly," he said. "Something must have happened. Or she's pretending everything is all right—and she's about to break."

According to Smith, Violet had continued to bring him food, cookies, and other treats while he worked. She never demanded anything of him. "She usually just knocks on the doorframe and says, 'You're doing wonderfully.' And then, she disappears down the hall."

Only once did Anna really think something was wrong with Violet.

They were in the nursery with Adam, changing him into a light blue onesie and doting over him. Neither could believe he was nearly two months old. He was already in the ninetieth percentile size-wise, and they made him believe he was incredibly smart and understood far more than he let on.

"He's our baby genius," Anna said, giggling as she raised him into the air.

"Just imagine what he'll be like at the wedding!" Violet agreed. "Maybe he can be your little ring bearer. Won't Daddy think he's so cute?"

Anna's smile fell off her face. Slowly, she shifted Adam into her arms and blinked at Violet, who continued to smile as though nothing was wrong. "Are you talking about Mom's wedding? The one next month?"

Violet blinked at her dully as though she wasn't sure what Anna was talking about. Anna had the strangest suspicion that Violet was talking about a very different wedding. The one she'd been engaged for. The one that hadn't happened.

"Of course," Violet sputtered.

"Because I don't think he'll be up for being a ring bearer," Anna said. "He won't be able to walk!" She adjusted her tone, making it childish and sweet again.

"Of course!" Violet repeated, wavering from foot to foot.

That evening, Anna met with her mother in her office. Julia looked frazzled, her hair in a giant knot atop her head, Smith's manuscript spread across the desk. Anna sat beside her, watching Julia's massive red pen wiggling across the pages, making edits and corrections. Once, she wrote a large "WHY" over an entire paragraph, which Anna found a little aggressive.

When Anna explained what had happened that afternoon with Violet, Julia frowned, forming a stack of wrinkles on her hairline. "She must have misspoken."

"I don't know," Anna offered. "It almost felt like, for a minute, she genuinely believed Adam would be the ring bearer at my wedding—to Dean."

"Maybe she meant a different wedding?" Julia tried. "I mean, everyone has noticed you and Smith are getting closer."

"We're just friends."

Julia rubbed her temples and returned her gaze to the manuscript. Massive shadows lurked beneath her eyes. This wasn't a good time.

"How is it going?" Anna asked, nodding toward the pages.

"Oh? I mean, fine. Mostly." Julia chewed on the edge of a pen absentmindedly, a habit she'd told Anna was disgusting. "I can't help but feel Smith has slowed down a little. As though he's distracted."

Heat crawled up Anna's throat. The last thing she

wanted was to get between Smith and her mother and their publishing schedule.

"Then again, there's nothing harder than writing the end of a book," Julia added, forcing a smile. "I'm sure he'll finish strong." A hint of doubt lingered in her voice and continued to echo in Anna's mind for hours later.

* * *

The day before Adam's two-month birthday, there was a knock on Anna's bedroom door. Smith and Luka were on the other side, Smith with a backpack filled with a picnic and Luka with a wide-eyed, tongue-lolling smile.

"Good morning!" Anna said. She was still wearing sweatpants and a tank top, and only half of her makeup was done, a result of Adam squawking in the middle of her routine.

"Do you have plans today?" Smith asked. "I need to get out of the house."

Anna hurried to dress, finish her makeup, and prepare a bag with Adam's many required accessories—diapers, wipes, bottles, and brightly colored distractions. She'd read that babies couldn't see very well during their first few months of life, which made the bright, blurry items all the more interesting.

With Adam wrapped across her chest, Anna followed Smith into the light of the late morning. It was mid-March and nearly sixty degrees, the air balmy as it shifted through the trees. In just a few weeks, the first shoots of green would burst from the soil.

"As you can see," Smith said, extending his arms, "it's impossible to stay indoors today."

Anna grinned from ear to ear. "What's the plan?"

It turned out that Smith didn't have a plan. He wanted to make up the day "by ear." Anna, whose days had fallen into a rhythm of Adam's schedule, relished the idea and promised herself to soak up every minute of spontaneity.

First up was coffee and croissants at the Nantucket Historic Café. They sat on the front patio and watched the sailboats shift across the sloshing water. Anna drank her coffee carefully as Adam slept on her chest, and Smith gave scraps of croissant to Luka. A married couple in their fifties approached, gushing about what a "beautiful family" they were.

"Your baby looks brand new," the woman said.

"Two months," Smith said proudly.

Anna's heart lifted. She realized this probably wasn't the first time people had seen the three of them (plus Luka) and considered them a family. Was this the kind of nourishing feeling she would have enjoyed with Dean? It was different, she decided.

After croissants and coffee, Smith suggested he take a turn with Adam. Anna helped him wrap the carrier over his shoulders and situate Adam against his chest. Smith was a natural, falling into a loose stride that didn't shake the baby too much. Luka shuffled along beside him. Anna's heart swelled.

They wandered through the Historic District, past restaurants that still hadn't opened for the tourism season, tourist shops that sold seashells and scarves, and the wedding dress shop where Julia had selected her gown for next month. Anna described the cut and color of the dress as best as she could, calling it a "modern-day take on Stevie Nicks, but a classier version."

Smith was intrigued. "You have a way with descriptions," he told Anna. "I noticed that the first time I googled your writing."

Anna's cheeks burned. As they hovered outside the wedding dress shop, she imagined herself entering in a year or two, a different engagement ring on her finger, toddler Adam at home with his stand-in father, Smith. Was it too much to hope for?

"What do you say?" Anna asked, her throat thick with fear. "Do you want to go to the wedding with me?"

Smith turned to look her straight in the eye. "I'd love to."

After they looped through the Historic District again, they returned to The Copperfield House to grab Anna's car. They secured Adam in his car seat, slipped into the front, and whizzed off to the opposite end of the island. Without a vehicle of his own, Smith had only seen areas of Nantucket in The Copperfield House's immediate vicinity, but with a car, he dove into the nooks and crannies, his eyes wide as he swallowed every view.

"Look at that," he whispered when Anna stopped the engine at a lookout.

The beach beyond was deserted, just a wide stretch of sand dunes that glinted beneath the March sunlight and surged against a dangerous, dark ocean.

"Growing up in the Midwest means I'm still not so sure about that water," Anna admitted. "I'm a strong swimmer, sure. But there's something about the ocean."

"Something we can't understand," Smith agreed.

As they watched the waves rush across the sands, a squawking flock of seagulls surged overhead. In the back seat of the car, Adam made a noise in his throat.

"It sounds like he's trying to answer them," Anna said with a laugh. "What are they saying, buddy?"

"They're saying they want our picnic," Smith joked, reaching for his backpack between his legs.

Smith unfurled what he'd packed: turkey and cheddar sandwiches with lettuce and tomato, pretzels, grapes, and dark chocolate. Anna took a small bite of her sandwich and closed her eyes, marveling at how wonderful it felt to be cared for. That was something Smith had never been allowed to feel as a child. Oh, she wished she could take that pain from his heart.

"I feel like you should know something," Smith said, his eyes still on the ocean.

Anna swirled with potentialities. Maybe Smith was planning to leave. Maybe Smith had met someone else—an islander whose stomach was flat. An islander who was uncomplicated.

Instead, he lent her the surprise of the year.

"I'm falling in love with you."

Anna's eyes filled with tears. The world around her blurred, the sand morphing into the sky, the ocean frothing into greens and blues. When Dean died, she didn't think anyone would ever love her again. Yet here she was, nearly a year later, with an aching heart and a fresh story.

Before Anna could answer, Smith went on. Apparently, he'd thought this through.

"You've been through a lot. You lost your fiancé, and then you had his baby. I want you to know I recognize that. And I don't want to push you into anything too quickly." Smith wrapped up his sandwich, clearly uninterested in food. "But I also want you to know I'm a patient person. I've been through enough to know that this sort of connection isn't common."

Anna folded her sandwich in its plastic wrap and

reached for his hand. They laced their fingers together as though they were two pieces of the same puzzle. She realized she'd felt this way from the moment she'd seen him on the beach, gazing up at the moon.

"I feel like we're at the beginning of something," she whispered. "Let's take it one step at a time."

Smith smiled. "Your mom thinks I need to get better at pacing in writing, anyway," he joked. "I might as well practice in real life."

Chapter Seventeen

The sunset over Nantucket was a sherbert smear of oranges, pinks, reds, and blues. Anna nursed Adam in her car, where she'd parked in the harbor, watching as Smith took photographs along the railing. It was nearly seven, nine hours into their "adventure day," and Anna felt light and happy, like a confident mother, a wonderful lover, and a good friend. There was nothing she couldn't do. Smith had even convinced her to contact a few of her recent clients, explaining that she'd just had a baby but that she was eager to join the workforce again in the summertime. There was always plenty to write about in Nantucket in the summer.

Adam finished nursing and fell back asleep. Overwhelmed with love, Anna worked slowly and diligently, scooping him back into his carrier and stepping into the evening. She joined Smith by the railing and wrapped her arm around him, swaying with him gently as they watched the night swallow up the day.

"I have a question," Smith said after a time. His tone was wistful. "Would you ever write about it?"

Anna frowned. "About what?"

"About Dean. About all of it." Smith pressed his lips together nervously.

"You mean, like a memoir?" Anna asked.

Smith shrugged.

Anna cradled Adam's head with her hand. "I don't know. I don't think so." She paused. "I think some things are too sacred to share."

A flicker of fear came over Smith's face. Immediately, Anna regretted what she'd said, thinking of her mother, of the book she and Smith were planning to publish. Smith was clearly having second thoughts about publishing something so revealing about himself, his family, and his mother.

As Anna searched her mind for a better answer, something to calm him down, Adam began to wail again. This cry was different, proof he needed a diaper change. "Shoot," she muttered, suddenly flailing between her worries for Smith and her worries for her baby. "I just ran out of wipes. I have to run into the store."

There was a mini-market three minutes from the dock, where sailors stocked up on supplies for their treks across the ocean. There had to be wipes there.

"Let me take him while you go," Smith said. His voice was nurturing and calm.

"Are you sure?"

"Of course. I'd do anything for this little guy."

Smith scooped Adam into his arms and stood still as Anna adjusted the carrier around him. Adam continued to wail with confusion and discomfort. It triggered her in a biological sense. She had to care for him.

Again, she thought of Smith's mother—who hadn't heard that call.

Anna fled the harbor and traced the sidewalk to the sailor's market. It was an unorganized disaster, with fruits and vegetables rolling around on the floor and unstocked aisles meant to boast bread and cereals. A woman smoked a cigarette out front and emerged only when she realized Anna wanted to buy something. She sniffed at Anna, accustomed to a different sort of clientele.

"Just these," Anna said, placing a package of wipes on the counter. It was a miracle she'd found them. In the distance, she could still hear Adam crying, and it made her stomach cramp.

Anna hurried back to the harbor, eager to tend to her son. But as she whipped around the corner, she realized Smith and Adam were no longer by themselves. Adam's cries were louder, sharper, as though he was warning her of something. Anna quickened her pace.

There was a woman with Smith and Adam. She waved her hands and cried out, and her blond hair was a violent web around her head. It took Anna a few blinks to realize it was Violet—unkempt, loud, and volatile. Her eyes showed too much of their whites.

As Anna neared them, she understood more and more of what Violet screamed. And it wasn't good.

"It shouldn't have been you! It was never meant to be you!"

Anna's stomach curdled. She ripped forward, so close that Adam's cries tore through her eardrum.

"Do you hear me? Do you understand?" Violet demanded.

Smith wore a pained expression. His hands were wrapped over Adam's ears, protecting him from Violet's rage.

"I understand," Smith was saying very quietly. "I know. It's too much."

Violet gasped with tears and fell forward, gripping her knees. "It wasn't supposed to happen like this." She hiccuped. "It's all wrong!"

Anna was at a loss. She alternated her gaze between Smith and Violet. Smith's eyes glinted with tears, and they coated his cheeks. Anna wanted to throw her arms around him. Before she could, Smith unbuckled Adam's carrier gently and gestured for Anna to take him back.

"I have to go," Smith said.

Anna sputtered. "Go? Where?"

Smith bowed his head toward the woman before them, who was crumpled in a heap, teetering on the brink of a mental abyss.

Anna wanted to tell Smith that Violet wasn't his responsibility and that they should call someone. A doctor. Her mother. Anyone else. But what good would that do? Violet was alone in the world. In many ways, Smith was just as alone. Perhaps he was the only one who could reach her.

"Violet?" Smith breathed, speaking to her the way he might a child. "Violet, will you come with me?"

Violet sniffled and rubbed her eyes. Anna held her baby tighter, wanting to translate as much love as she could to remind Adam she would always be there for him. But there was so much she couldn't know about the future. What if she got sick? What if something happened? What if Adam grew up alone?

As Smith led Violet away from Nantucket Harbor, they slipped away from the boardwalk and drifted onto the shadowed sands. Anna watched them go, mystified.

Again, she searched her mind for some sign of Dean, asking for his advice. "What should I do about your poor mother?" But Dean, wherever he was, couldn't hear her. They were on their own.

Chapter Eighteen

Violet couldn't remember how she'd gotten to the Nantucket Harbor. Much like the rest of her grief-soaked days, time had become foggy and amorphous, streaked with tears.

It had all begun that morning. She'd been on the phone with the Nantucket flower shop, ordering a heaping selection of gorgeous bouquets for the reception tables at Julia's upcoming wedding. She'd felt prim and organized and thought by imitating wedding planners on television, she'd become one. Maybe, she'd thought, she could actually make this her business again. Maybe she would never have to be an accountant again—a career she'd only done to help pay the bills.

When Violet got off the phone with the flower shop, she jumped on Facebook to write to the reception venue. It had been innocuous and just another task. But she hadn't expected to see what she'd seen right there on her feed. Facebook should have a "warning" label.

One of her friends from Dayton had tagged herself and her husband in a photo album. In it, her friend wore a beautiful magenta dress that Violet was pretty sure she'd helped pick out. Her husband was in a suit and a cowboy hat, typical of his style. Just seeing them again made Violet pang with homesickness. She'd abandoned Ohio without a second thought—driving halfway across the continent. Adam had been her only hope.

But as Violet clicked through the photo album, a sickly dread took hold of her. Everyone in the photos was dressed to the nines and smiled deliriously. It was clear from not even halfway through the album that the event was a wedding. Violet knew nearly every single guest. They were fathers and mothers of Dean's friends; they were old neighbors, even some who'd moved away; they were relations of Larry.

And then, Violet found the bride and groom.

It shouldn't have come as such a surprise. It shouldn't have felt like a knife through the stomach. After all, Larry and Hazel had been back together since last April—nearly a year ago. They called each other "soul mates." Marriage was always in the cards.

But Violet was a fool. She'd half-believed that leaving Dayton behind meant that Hazel and Larry no longer existed. Yet here they were, stronger than ever. Happy.

They looked beautiful together. Larry had lost weight, presumably because he'd joined Hazel's gym, and he'd gotten his teeth whitened (something he'd always said was frivolous before). Hazel wore a barely-there wedding dress that Violet couldn't have even pulled off back in her twenties. In one of the photos, they pressed cake against each other's mouths and cackled.

There was a video, too. Because she was a masochist, Violet pressed play and listened as Hazel talked about the "grief" that had brought them back together again. "It's never too late to build the life of your dreams," she said.

After watching the video, Violet blacked out. She'd come to only moments ago, in fact, finding herself guided home along the sands by the young man who was the same age as her son. What was his name? He looked familiar. Violet stumbled and reached out to take his arm. Tears stained her cheeks, and her shoes were covered in sand.

"He married her," Violet rasped, surprising herself. "He really did it."

"Let's get you inside," the young man urged. "It's cold out here."

Violet only realized how frigid she was when she got back inside. Her teeth clacked together, and her toes lost their feeling as she mounted the stairs. The young man, whose name she was pretty sure was Smith, opened the door to her bedroom and guided her to the edge of her bed. "I'm going to make you some tea," he said. "Sit here, okay? And focus on your breathing."

Violet stared into space for several minutes as the feeling returned to her toes and fingers. There were sounds in the massive house around her—footsteps and murmured words. She was fearful they were talking about her. That's right. She was in The Copperfield House—a massive Victorian on the beach of Nantucket. She was here, where her grandson lived. Here, where Anna's entire family looked at her as though she were a thorn in their side. She'd come to Nantucket thinking she was worthless and unloveable—and they'd confirmed it.

Smith returned with a big mug of tea, toast with peanut butter and jam, and a big stack of chocolate chip cookies. Violet's stomach pulsed with hunger. She hadn't eaten at all today, not that she remembered. She took a sip of tea and closed her eyes, trying to calm her anxious heart.

"How did you find me?" Violet asked, lifting her eyes to look at Smith. He sat at the chair by the desk, drinking tea. He looked pale and frightened, and it terrified Violet to think she'd caused it.

"You found me," Smith offered.

Violet was terrified to ask about that. She didn't want to hear how crazy she really was.

"Who married whom?" Smith asked then, saving her from her swirling thoughts.

"My ex-husband," Violet said. "Ten years ago, he had an affair with Dean's science teacher. After Dean died, they got back together, and they got married over the weekend."

Violet said it flatly, as though she spoke about something simple like the weather. She hoped this would force her to get over it.

Empathy echoed back in Smith's eyes. "That's awful. I'm so sorry."

Warmth flooded through Violet's chest. She sipped more tea and stretched out her toes, grateful to feel them again. "I shouldn't act out like that. I'm a grown woman."

"You've been through tremendous stress," Smith reminded her. "Sometimes, the body reacts to certain stimuli without asking permission."

Violet remembered that Smith had come from a troubled background. His mother had been abusive, and he'd had to raise his half brother himself. When she'd first learned this via the gossip channels of The Copperfield House, something in her heart had shattered, and she'd pledged herself to make Smith's life a little bit easier, to add an extra layer of comfort to his day. She'd found herself cooking him pasta and delivering little treats. Each time he opened his door, she caught herself hoping that the man on the other side would be her son. It was a form of magical thinking, she knew. But each time, Smith had smiled gratefully, thanking her. And a piece of her "mama" heart had brightened.

"I just can't figure out what I'm doing here." Violet surprised herself with her honesty. "I adore baby Adam, but I know Anna needs to create her own rhythm. She doesn't want me hovering over her shoulder every few minutes."

"Anna loves that you're here," Smith told him gently. "She wants you to be a part of Adam's life."

Violet laughed wryly. "I don't know if that's true."

Smith crossed his ankles. "Maybe it wasn't always true. But I assure you, it is, now."

Violet's heart lifted. Abstractly, she wondered if Smith was accustomed to dealing with women like herself if, once upon a time, his mother had been similarly disheveled, wandering around without comprehension of where or who she was.

"I really am so sorry for all you've lost," Smith told her, his voice cracking.

"You've lost so much, too. I know that."

Smith lowered his gaze. Something in his face made Violet imagine what he'd looked like twenty years ago—age six, with no one to care for him. She fought the urge to hug him.

"Sometimes, I wonder if it's too late for me," Smith said. "If I've gone through too much pain to properly love anyone or really let someone in."

An image of Anna at Dean's funeral floated through

Violet's mind. She'd been red-nosed and pale-cheeked, wavering on her feet as though on the verge of collapse. Nobody had known she was carrying Dean's baby. Violet remembered being jealous of the girl, knowing she would have to move on from this one day. That she was too young not to. Violet had been a fool. That wasn't something you got over. You carried it with you forever, like a tumor beneath your heart.

"I guess you've heard about my mother?" Smith said then.

"Bits and pieces. I know you're writing about her." Violet stuttered. "Has it been helping? Writing it, I mean."

Smith swallowed and shook his head. "I thought it would help. I thought it would get it all out of my system. But instead, it's forced me to relive every harrowing detail. And it's really messed with my psyche. I find myself avoiding it more and more. Trying to block it out."

Violet nodded, sensing their shared pain swimming in the air between them. "When did your mother die, Smith?"

Smith's eyes were rimmed with red. He set his mug on the desk, clasped his hands, and pressed them over his lips as though he wanted to keep the truth to himself.

And then, Violet heard herself echo the same words she'd told Dean a long time ago when all she'd wanted to do was keep him safe.

"You know, you can talk to me about anything, right?"

Smith's eyes lifted to find hers again. They echoed his grief. But they dared to dream of a future. Of a home.

Chapter Nineteen

All evening, Adam was fussy. It was as though he sensed the turmoil in the house and the worry in Anna's heart. Anna did everything in her mother's playbook: nursing, burping, walking, and driving. Still, Adam wailed. Around one thirty in the morning, when Adam finally drifted off to sleep, Anna collapsed on her bed, rubbed her eyes, and checked her phone for signs from Smith. There was nothing.

> ANNA: Hey! Just checking in. How did it go with Violet?

Ordinarily, Smith was a night owl. No text was too late. But tonight, Smith didn't even read the message. Anna frowned and rubbed her chest, where a knot was growing. Knowing what was happening on the other side of the house was impossible.

What was important, she reminded herself, was that Smith had told her he was falling in love. They'd agreed to take things slow.

Somehow, Anna drifted off to sleep and awoke with a

lurch at six thirty. Someone was knocking on her door. Still in her clothes from yesterday, Anna waded through the darkness and opened the door to find Violet before her, dressed in the coat she'd come in. She looked sheepish and under-slept, but her face was no longer marred with the strain and fear of yesterday. She looked completely present.

"Hey, honey."

"Violet!" Anna stepped back to usher Violet inside. She didn't want to wake up anyone else down the hall.

Inside Anna's room, Violet gazed down at a sleeping Adam and touched his arm tenderly with the tip of her finger. Anna took this opportunity to check for a text from Smith. Nothing.

"I want to apologize for yesterday," Violet said softly, without taking her eyes off Adam. "I was under tremendous stress, and I lost myself. I don't want you to worry. I called my psychiatrist back in Ohio and asked about medication and future care. And he's going to welcome me back with open arms tomorrow afternoon."

Anna's jaw dropped. She'd once dreamed of Violet's departure. Very suddenly, it terrified her. "Violet, you can get a doctor here," she reminded her. "Whatever's going on, we can help you through." She gestured vaguely toward Adam. "Your grandson is here. And he already loves you."

Violet's eyes sparkled with tears. "I appreciate you saying that, honey. I do."

"It's true."

Violet tilted her head as though trying to process what Anna said. Her shoulders drooped. "Other things are waiting for me in Ohio. Things I have to do. People I have to speak with." She swallowed. "Larry dumped me last year after Dean died. I've been too embarrassed to say it. But he married over the weekend, forcing me to acknowledge the truth.

"Larry and I haven't spoken at all since last spring," Violet said. "I still have a few things at the house. And more than that, I want to forgive him. I don't want to carry around this hatred for the rest of my life. It's a baggage too heavy for one woman on her own."

Anna's voice wavered. "You're not alone, Violet." She then closed the distance between them and wrapped her arms around her. As Violet shook with sorrow, Anna planted her chin on her shoulder and said, "You always have a place here. Call me as soon as you get to Ohio. We can figure this out together."

Violet's muscles loosened against Anna's fingers. Their hug parted, and Violet wiped her cheeks with the sleeve of her coat. "I have a big drive ahead of me," she said, gazing back at Adam. "Wish me luck."

Anna stood at her bedroom window and watched Violet drive away from The Copperfield House. She felt like she was coming undone.

After Adam woke up, Anna fed him with tears streaking her cheeks. She then cleaned herself up, put Adam in his carrier, and headed for the door that separated the two halves of the house. Up the stairs, she found herself before Smith's door, listening for the familiar panting of Luka. The sound of emptiness within was like a roar.

"Smith?" Anna rapped her knuckles on his door as her blood pressure spiked. "Smith, are you there?"

A feeling of dread crawled up her stomach and back. She couldn't wait a moment more and tore open the door to discover his room empty. His laptop and books no longer filled the desk in a wild array that, she'd thought, indicated his genius. His suitcase and backpack weren't in the closet. And most importantly, Luka no longer lay at the foot of Smith's bed, waiting for him to wake up.

Anna collapsed at the edge of Smith's bed and cried into her palms. None of it made any sense. Why had Smith and Violet decided to skip town on the very same day? What had they said to each other after Smith had led her away from the harbor?

Anna suspected that it was all tied up in Smith's memories of his mother. Violet's difficulties drudged up the past. And maybe, being at The Copperfield House had become too painful for Smith—reopening old wounds.

That or Smith had decided he just wasn't ready for whatever "love" existed between them. Maybe the minute he'd said "love" to Anna, he'd regretted it and known to get away. That was what men did, right? They avoided commitment.

Before she left his bedroom, Anna got up the nerve to call Smith. She imagined him on the ferry, the wind making his black hair flip and rush past his ears. There was no answer. When she called again, it went straight to voicemail as though he'd blocked her.

Somehow, Anna got herself to Scarlet's bedroom door. Her arms were strained from holding Adam's carrier, and her stomach was empty and gurgling. When Scarlet opened it, her face immediately transformed from one of recent slumber to one of concern.

"Are you okay?" Scarlet ushered Anna inside and closed the door behind her.

Immediately, Anna burst into tears. In the mirror, she saw herself as a mottled tomato, weeping into Scarlet's shoulder. Mercifully, Adam remained asleep in his carrier. Anna didn't want him to see her like this, even if he couldn't make sense of it.

Scarlet ordered Anna to sit down on her bed. From beneath the bedframe, she procured several varieties of chocolate, a bottle of wine, and crackers. "Pick your poison," she said.

Anna checked her phone. "It's only nine!"

"And? Life is hard any time of the day!" Scarlet raised her eyebrows, then filled two clean coffee mugs with red wine. Anna remembered there were plenty of baby bottles in the fridge for Adam to drink from later. She also remembered she was only twenty-four years old. Maybe, in another reality, she would have met her friends for a mimosa-filled brunch in Seattle. Maybe she would have been carefree.

"He's gone," Anna admitted after a sip.

"What?" Scarlet demanded. Her voice was etched with anger.

"Smith. I just went to his room. He took everything."

Scarlet looked flabbergasted. "What? Are you serious?" She shot to her feet and glared out the window as though that would reveal Smith's secrets. "Tell me everything."

Anna tried her best to articulate every beat of yesterday's nearly perfect date. She spoke of the conversations they'd had, of Smith telling her he was falling in love with her, of the people who'd approached and called them a gorgeous family. She finished with Violet panicking in the harbor and Smith taking her home.

"She always took care of him," Anna recalled. "She brought him pasta and little treats, things like that."

"I remember," Scarlet said. "My mom thought it was

sweet. Like Violet wanted to adopt him because he never really had a mother."

Anna wrinkled her nose. "It is sweet, I guess. I don't know. I just can't figure out what they said to one another that pushed them both out the door."

Scarlet groaned and took a swig of wine.

"I was stupid to think it could be that easy," Anna whispered, looking out the window, where a March rain splattered. "I should have guarded my heart. I should have kept to myself."

"No," Scarlet insisted, her hand in a fist. "He's smarter than this. He's a writer. He knows words have meanings. He knows what he's done." She snarled. "We're going to find him, Anna."

But Anna knew better than to fight for something when it was straining to get away from you. She shook her head and looked down at Adam, reminding herself of the only thing she was put on the earth to fight for.

Chapter Twenty

It was true that Smith's writing had dwindled over the previous few weeks. Julia had chased him for assignments, reminding him that if they didn't finish the first draft soon, there was no hope of an autumn release. Already, Bernard had finished his first draft and was working on his edits, setting his book up to be the "release of the holiday season." Julia ached for Smith, for what he was throwing away. Didn't he know he could have been someone great?

Maybe not everyone reached their potential, Julia reminded herself. Maybe Smith would be one of the ones who slipped through her fingers.

And this was proven true on day three after he left when he returned his advance. Julia wrote him an email immediately, explaining that, legally, he didn't have to do that. That the money was his. But he didn't respond.

In the wake of Smith's departure, initial spring temperatures shot back down the wintery ones, capturing everyone back in The Copperfield House for more rounds of tea and cozy movie nights. Anna wore sweats continually and wandered around the house glumly with Adam on her chest. Julia tried her best to bring Anna's spirits up, including her in last-minute wedding plans and dragging her to her final wedding dress fittings.

"She tried to love again," Charlie said over dinner one night, "and it failed. I can only imagine this has drudged up even more pain from losing Dean. One loss always brings up another."

Julia was surprised at how much she missed Violet. Ever since their trip to Manhattan, she'd genuinely enjoyed Violet's presence, grateful for her whimsy, her wedding planning, and her clear love of Adam. She was just as much Adam's grandmother as Julia was, and Julia found herself panging with guilt, wondering if they'd had a hand in pushing her out the door. Her crimes had been minimal. She'd bought too much baby gear and given too much parenting advice. But they'd fallen in love with her. They wanted her in the Copperfield family.

Four nights after Violet and Smith left The Copperfield House, Julia was up late, editing Bernard's manuscript. She found herself laughing aloud at his prose, grateful that he'd found his sense of humor again.

A knock on the door brought Anna inside. Unlike usual, she didn't have Adam with her. "Scarlet offered to babysit," she explained. "I worked out, shaved my legs, and listened to a podcast. It was wonderful."

Julia laughed and twirled in her office chair. After two and a half months of motherhood, Anna had begun to look more and more like herself—younger, fresher, healthier. It was terrible, the toll pregnancy took on your body. Julia had mostly blocked out her three pregnancies and the terror she'd gone through trying to fit back into a size four. She'd felt professional, personal, and husband pressure. Ugh.

"I wanted to tell you something," Anna announced. "Something I remember from that last day with Smith."

Julia cocked her head. She sensed a confession.

"He asked me, um, if I would ever write about Dean," Anna stuttered. "If I would ever, you know, write about his tragedy and giving birth to his baby nine months later. And without thinking, I told him I thought some things are too sacred to write about." Anna grimaced and clasped her hands.

Julia bowed her head. Already, she'd sensed this had something to do with it but hadn't found a way to articulate it to Anna. There were some things words couldn't express fully.

"It's not your fault, honey," she assured her. "I think Smith was already getting cold feet about doing the memoir."

"But I pushed him," Anna said.

"No. I don't think so," Julia insisted. "Writing about his past was too painful for him. I think, in our genetic makeup, it's almost impossible to betray our mothers like that, no matter how cruel or awful they were. I feel bad for even allowing him to go after it." Julia grimaced as guilt swelled in her chest. Had she really wanted to push Smith for her publishing house's profit? Was that really what she was all about?

Julia had to take a cold, hard look at her motivations. She had to remember to exhibit empathy in everything she did. Otherwise, she was no better than Marcia Conrad.

Anna's face echoed with empathy. After a thoughtful pause, she added, "Smith never told me what happened to his mother."

"He never reached that part of the book," Julia said. "Your guess is as good as mine."

Chapter Twenty-One

Anna and Scarlet took Adam to his next doctor's appointment, where they learned that Adam was healthy and happy and still far bigger than most babies his age. Anna laughed, saying, "I can already feel it in my arms! He's growing!"

To this, the doctor said, "You'll get stronger." And Anna felt this was a wonderful metaphor for motherhood. That when things got harder and heavier, you were simply required to tackle them. And you did that because of the strength of your love.

After the doctor's appointment, they met Grandma Greta, Julia, Aunt Ella, Aunt Catherine, and Aunt Alana at a downtown café. They were coming from Julia's final fitting for her wedding dress, which had made them all weep with joy. Julia showed Anna a final photograph, wherein Julia had her hands on her hips, and Aunt Ella and Aunt Alana were on either side, imitating Charlie's Angels. Anna cackled and returned the phone. Out the window, a late-March sun warmed the frozen ground, and the coffee shop began to set up tables and chairs on the outside patio. It was nearly time to begin again.

When Anna returned to The Copperfield House that afternoon, she put Adam in his crib and checked her email. As she'd promised Smith she would, she'd been in contact with several editors, most of whom had written back. "Send me pitches!" one said. "I love your writing. We'd be happy to publish you again."

As Anna typed a response, her email dinged with another message. Thinking it was an editor, she clicked back to her inbox.

FROM: Smith Watson

Anna jumped from her chair so quickly that it fell back behind her and rattled on the ground. She blinked several times, daring it to be a mirage. It had been over a week since he'd left. Already, he'd turned into her ghost, haunting her dreams.

Dear Anna,

I know you hate me. You're not the only one. Ever since I left last week, I've marveled at the pain I can cause myself, which I do again and again. But I've also ached at the pain I know I've caused you. It's been a long time since I opened myself up to something so real. And I'd forgotten that something like that ultimately paves the way to hardship and turmoil.

You deserve an explanation. Even if you never want to see me again, I'll give you that.

For many months now, I've been plagued with nightmares of my mother. Some of them are memories of her yelling, fighting, and throwing things. But in others, she's sobbing on the ground, asking me why I did what I did. Asking me why I didn't love her enough.

The truth is, I've always loved my mother. The fact

that she didn't show her love when I was a child made me crave it even more. It was an endless cycle I thought I'd escaped when I fled for Brooklyn. But then, there I was, writing page after page about her, about what she'd done to me. When your mother said she wanted to publish the memoir and bring me to The Copperfield House to finish it, I thought that gave validity to my suffering. But in actuality, these events only emphasized my pain.

On that last evening before I left, I sat with Violet for ages. She told me about how devastated she's been since her son's death, and I told her how empty I've felt since I left my mother behind. I've never found a way to forgive her... but I've also never found a way to forgive myself.

Violet losing Dean like that forced me to reckon with the nature of time. My mother won't be around forever. More than that, I won't be around forever. We're two individuals floating through space on a big rock called Earth. Any novels I publish won't be "remembered" in the grand history of all things. I'm not James Joyce or Sylvia Plath. I'm generally no one—except for a very broken man who was once a boy.

In that way, I knew I couldn't publish that memoir. It would destroy far more than it would build up. And I don't want to make a mockery of my past. I don't want to commodify it. So much of it is me, you know?

Talking to Violet forced me to remember, too, that I disappeared from my mother's life. I never gave her the chance to realize what she'd done. I wasn't even sure if she deserved it. But I figured, after ten years away, I had a right to know what she'd say.

And I'm so glad I came back to Pennsylvania to find out.

I'm writing to you from the hotel down the street from my

mother's house—the same house in which I was raised, where she burned me with the skillet and where she sobbed herself to sleep and I worried she wouldn't wake up. All of that is true. But it's also the hotel down the street from the house in which I played with my stuffed animals, taught myself to cook pasta, and received a bike for my sixth birthday. The good memories are tied up with the bad. And my memoir wasn't allowing any space for the good ones. How is that fair?

My little brother is here at the hotel with me. He's twelve now, which blows my mind, and he's showing me his new video game, which was a present from Mom's newest boyfriend.

Mom seemed okay. A little tired, maybe. But softer. Gentler. She told me losing me forced her to go to therapy, where she was prescribed medicine for bipolar disorder. Things have still been up and down for her since then, but she's had more ups than downs. A blessing. I sobbed when she told me that. I'd always known something was wrong, something I couldn't name.

And I knew then why I couldn't write that memoir. I still love this woman. I always will.

I asked her about my half brother, Freddie. About whether she was up to raising him. And she burst into tears. She told me she's so tired. That she's on a constant quest for love that has nothing to do with her love for Freddie. I went into Freddie's room after that and asked him about his upbringing, about whether Mom was nice to him or not. Freddie said she yelled. And in his eyes, I saw a reflection of my own childhood.

And downstairs, I offered to take Freddie home with me. Wherever "home" turns out to be. I hope I'm up to the task of showing him the kind of love he's been missing.

Maybe my mother just doesn't have the capacity to show it, no matter what her medication is. What a curse that must be for her.

I'm so grateful for my capacity to feel. I feel so much about you, which I've already shared. I don't blame you if you've lost those feelings. That's the nature of time.

This has turned into a long-winded email. I wouldn't blame you if you haven't made it to the end.

Just know that I'm thinking of you. And that I'd love to meet again when you're ready.

Yours,

Smith

Not long after Anna finished reading the letter, she lay back on her bed and stared at the crack in the ceiling, listening as the early spring winds surged across the house and made the foundation quiver. Her breasts were tender, and it was nearly time to feed Adam again. She groaned and curled up in a ball, thinking about the sacrifice of motherhood and love.

There was a knock.

"Hello?"

Anna sat up as Julia entered her room, white as a sheet.

"Are you okay?" Anna whispered. They'd already received so much bad news. What was next?

"I just heard from Smith," Julia said. "He pitched me a new novel. He says he's already written more than half of it."

Anna furrowed her brow. "A novel? Not a memoir this time?"

Julia shook her head as her eyes glinted. "But he said it takes place in a so-called Victorian castle on the beach of Nantucket. And he wants to finish it in time to publish it in late autumn.

A slow smile traced across Anna's face. "Do you think he'll make it?"

Julia's face glowed. "I've always had a good feeling about him."

"Me too."

Chapter Twenty-Two

The first thing Violet learned when she reached Dayton was that Larry and Hazel were headed to Florida—probably forever. It was time to leave Ohio behind. Violet's best friend of ten years explained this tentatively over rosé that first evening, her fingertips pressed hard on the tabletop. "I think they want to start over," she said. "And I guess I can't blame them."

Violet inhaled and exhaled through the pain of this news, watching it affect her heart and dissipate, much like a tide rising and falling. She reminded herself this was hardly new information. Larry had always idealized Florida, calling it "heaven on earth." When Dean selected Seattle as his new home, Larry was mystified. "Of all the places in the world, why would you go somewhere cold and rainy?" Dean, who'd never taken anything badly, had laughed that off.

"I need to talk to him," Violet said to her best friend, swirling her wine in her glass. "I packed up the night of the funeral and never looked back."

After wine, Violet returned to her apartment near the

mall, where she'd continued to pay rent since her abrupt departure in December. Despite three months of abandonment, the apartment was hardly dusty. The same sweater she'd worn the night before she'd left was slung over the kitchen chair, and a newspaper from December 24th was spread across the counter. It was like entering a time machine.

Violet had put three framed photographs on the mantel—one of Dean and Anna, another of Dean with their old family dog, and another of herself, Dean, and Larry. Her heart panged with sorrow. Slowly, she removed the family photograph and tried to remember the specifics of the day it had been taken. She was pretty sure she'd forced Larry to wear that button-down. She'd thought it went better with her dress.

It was bizarre, the things you remembered. She told herself not to take issue with the little things later on (and to let "future Larry" wear whatever he dang well pleased for the photographs). She promised herself to take pleasure in the mundane. You never knew how much time you had left.

After Violet settled in and drank a glass of water, she texted Anna that she'd made it. Anna responded seconds later with several photographs of Adam, which immediately warmed her heart. Although Adam hadn't initially looked like Dean as a baby, he'd begun to show off Dean's features here and there—in his dimples and wrinkling his nose. Seeing this was just as wonderful as it was heartbreaking.

When Violet got up the nerve, she texted Larry to say she was back. Could they talk?

LARRY: You're back.

> LARRY: I was worried, Violet. I know I don't have a right to be. But I was, anyway.
>
> LARRY: Do you want to come by the house tomorrow afternoon?
>
> LARRY: Hazel won't be here.

When Violet read that final text, "Hazel won't be here," a shiver ran up and down her spine. Had Larry texted something similar to Hazel back when they'd had their secret affair? *"Violet won't be here. Don't worry. (Winky face emoji)."*

But Violet had logistic questions regarding the house. And she wanted to look Larry in the eye and say something—something about Dean. About all the love she still had in her heart for their family. It seemed essential to her healing process. And when she explained this to her psychiatrist the following morning, he agreed wholeheartedly. "You have to listen to your instincts. More often than not, they're right."

Violet's psychiatrist prescribed her medication that would calm her moods and keep her stable. But his biggest piece of advice was to *"be around people who love and respect you."* Violet's first thought was Anna—and Smith. Her throat swelled.

An hour before Violet planned to meet Larry at the house, Violet called Smith. They'd exchanged numbers on that last fateful night in The Copperfield House, promising to stay in touch as they fielded their separate problems. Smith answered on the third ring and listened intently as she described what she was about to do.

"That's your house, too," he reminded her. "Go in with your head held high."

Violet asked Smith about his mother, about what it had been like to see her again. Smith said he'd tell her later. "Don't worry about me," he urged.

"I'm a mother," Violet responded. "All I do is worry."

As Violet mounted the front steps of the house, all she could think about was the day they'd bought it. She'd been twenty years old; it had been more than half her life ago. Bill Clinton had still been president. There hadn't been a war.

And on that day, Larry had wrapped his arms around her, lifted her into the air, and said, "Baby, let's make a family here."

Violet rapped at the door, then rang the doorbell, realizing she'd never had to do that at her own house before. After a moment's pause, she turned the knob and entered. After all, her early wedding planning and later accounting work had paid for much of the mortgage. This foyer tile was just as much her foyer tile as his.

But she promised herself not to be petty.

There was a creak on the staircase. Violet raised her chin and watched as Larry, a more athletic Larry with brighter teeth—descended. He wore a pair of jeans and a white T-shirt, and if she wasn't mistaken, she was pretty sure there was foundation on a cut on his chin. But it was still her husband. It was still the same old Larry she'd always known.

Even the wedding band on his fourth finger looked similar to the one he'd worn for her.

Larry extended his arms. His eyes were filled with questions. Should they hug? Violet crossed her arms in response. There was no reason they needed to parade down old territory. Too much had happened.

"It's really good to see you," Larry said finally, letting his arms fall. "You look amazing."

Violet knew that the sea air of Nantucket had done her some good. She was tanner, too. And the long walks on the beach, the grandmother kisses, and Greta's food had done wonders. Even thinking of it now, she panged with homesickness for her new life.

"So do you," Violet said, as her throat filled with sorrow.

Larry spread his fingers through his hair. He looked nervous, like a kid. And then, he gestured toward the dining room and suggested they sit down. Violet followed him in to find a FOR SALE sign on the tabletop. She was grateful her friend had told her about the sale. She could play it cool now.

"I wanted to tell you in person that we're moving to Florida," Larry said.

"I see." Violet sat at the dining room table, remembering it was an antique from her mother's side of the family. Could she have it shipped to Nantucket? She imagined Adam eating roast beef sandwiches there, listening as Violet told him stories about his father.

"Of course, fifty percent of the sale will go to you," Larry said.

Violet nodded. She could use that to buy a small house in Nantucket or an apartment in the Historic District. An apartment suited her just fine. She'd never cared for lawn maintenance, anyway.

Larry still seemed flustered, probably because she still hadn't said much. So he added, "Maybe you heard. We got married."

Violet was surprised at how little that statement impacted her. She smiled. "I'm happy you're happy."

Larry stuttered. "Thank you. Yeah. I don't know. I feel like the past year, I've just been reeling. Wandering through my life. Grieving." He finally sat across from her and crossed his hands over the table. He looked reflective and old. Violet thought he looked more like his father than he ever had before.

"Violet, I should have been there for you," Larry blurted. "Neither of us should have had to carry that alone. And instead, I burrowed myself away. I hate myself for that."

Larry sniffled and went on. "If you're up for it, I'd love to talk on the phone sometimes," he said. "I want to talk about Dean with the only other person who really knows him. I want to share memories. I don't want to think he's just gone like that." He snapped his fingers.

"That's all I want, too." Violet was surprised at how open Larry was being. He'd had nearly a year to think about this, she supposed.

And they'd both made their way to a similar conclusion.

All they wanted was to continue loving their son. And they had to do that together if only to ensure the love remained strong and not forgotten.

Soon, Violet revealed the newest photos of baby Adam and watched as Larry melted into himself with gladness.

"He's got that dimple Dean used to have!" he cried.

Violet dried her eyes with her sleeve, remembering Larry cradling Dean in the living room, both of them asleep as a sporting event raged on the television. "You have to come out and see him," she said. "He's just as much your grandson as he is mine."

Larry passed the phone across the table and tilted his head. "Does that mean you're going back to Nantucket?"

Violet raised her eyebrows. "I think so."

Violet gave a brief description of the previous few months—of her frazzled nature, of driving Anna crazy, of finding a rhythm, of meeting a new friend named Smith.

"He never had anyone to worry about him," Violet said softly, thinking again of Smith's soft, wounded gaze. "Can you imagine what that would be like?"

Larry shook his head. "All my mother ever did was worry about where I was and what I would be."

"Mine, too. And we did the same for Dean."

Larry extended his legs beneath the table, and his ankles popped and creaked, just as they'd always done. Violet suppressed a smile. She imagined herself and Larry sitting down for dinner in ten or twenty years, talking about the good old times, their bones creaking. She imagined the pain of losing Dean to be a far-off star, ever-present, shining over them.

When Violet felt she'd stayed long enough, she and Larry walked back into the front yard and pushed the FOR SALE sign into the grass. They high-fived after that, laughing. "Let's get rid of this old place," Violet joked.

She knew she had a huge task ahead of her. Dean's room was filled with memories, just waiting for someone to go through. But after a year, so much turmoil, and newly prescribed medication, Violet felt ready for anything. It was the beginning of a new journey.

Chapter Twenty-Three

Anna had been engaged to Dean for fewer than twenty-four hours. Being the dreamer she was, Anna had planned an entire wedding during that time—all the way down to the fine details, the hors d'oeuvres, the place settings, and the song they would dance to. These fantasies, incredibly, would remain in Anna's mind forever. That was the marvelous nature of memories. And if she ever married again, she would opt for different plans, different details. The initial ones would always belong to her and Dean.

Smith had been gone for nearly a month. The days had stretched out strangely, becoming a rhythm of baby needs, writing tasks, and helping Greta and her mother around the house. Emails with Smith had punctuated her days, coming almost nightly, usually at around one or two. Having an email correspondence like this reminded her of Jane Austen romances. It gave new meaning to their initial conversation a month ago, in which they'd said they wanted to take things "slow." "I'll show you slow," they seemed to say.

But today was Julia's wedding to Charlie. And a part of Anna—the romantic part—ached for Smith to return to Nantucket and be her date. She knew it was complicated back in Pennsylvania. Smith was up to his ears in logistics, adopting his brother. But she needed him here.

Anna woke up early to a squeaking, smiling baby. Adam was three months old, with a plump belly and dark dimples. Her love for him overflowed.

Anna got Adam ready for the morning and walked him downtown to Violet's new apartment, which she rented from an older islander couple who usually rented it out to tourists for ridiculously high rates. Lucky for Violet, the couple wanted a long-term renter they could trust (for a lower rate), and the Copperfields were more than willing to advocate for her. Essentially, she was one of them.

Violet opened the door as Anna approached, hurrying to lift Adam from his stroller and smother him with kisses.

"Thank you for babysitting this morning," Anna said, smiling.

"Of course! I'm always happy to. Just remember, I have to be up at the venue by eleven thirty. The life of a wedding planner is exciting!" Violet said, wheeling the stroller deeper into her brightly lit apartment. Already, she had a "baby area" set up in the corner of her living room, where she'd stocked plenty of modern baby books. "Knowledge is power," she'd said several times, which both irritated Anna and made her laugh. Violet's love was powerful. And she was grateful for it.

"His little suit is just down here." Anna squatted to retrieve the adorable suit and tiny black shoes. "I don't know if he'll like the shoes. He's never worn any before. But Mom and I couldn't resist buying them."

Violet hung up the suit and clasped her hands. "Have a wonderful morning. Adam and I will see you later."

Before Anna left Violet's apartment, she hesitated, her hand lingering on the doorknob. Via email, Smith had expressed his tremendous affection for Violet—even saying that he'd begun to think of her as family. "It's easy for someone like me to latch onto family," he'd explained. "Because I never had one before."

Anna wondered if Violet knew when Smith was coming back. She searched her smile for secrets but found nothing. Her heart sank. Maybe it wasn't time yet.

The women of The Copperfield House were gathered in the living room. Love songs purred from the Bluetooth speaker, and satin robes were donned, glistening as they rushed from the kitchen and back again to pour more mimosas. Anna took several glances at herself in the mirror in the hall, noting that she'd lost quite a bit of the baby weight. She felt youthful and athletic, probably from carrying Adam around. She'd become stronger than ever.

Aunt Alana turned on a classic French song, dancing with her eyes closed, shimmying her hips. "Follow my lead, ladies!" she ordered.

Heaving with laughter, Scarlet, Anna, Ivy, Laura, and Julia tried to imitate Alana, whose ex-supermodel tendencies outrivaled their moves. Greta was far too sensible to even try. She just shook her head and sipped her mimosa, her eyes on Alana—the daughter she'd never fully understood.

Not long afterward, Rachel, Anna's little sister, came downstairs, yawning. She still attended the University of Michigan in Ann Arbor and was fresh-faced and innocent in her satin robe. She wrapped her arms around their mother and said, "You're the prettiest bride in the world." And Julia knelt her head upon Rachel's and thanked her. Anna's heart ached, knowing that her relationship with Julia was far different from Rachel's.

She wondered what another child would be like. How could anyone else come between her and Adam? It boggled her mind that her love for Adam could ever be doubled. But that was what motherhood was.

True to form, Grandma Greta made sure everyone ate enough for lunch. "I won't have any of you forgetting to eat," she said, bringing out salads, sandwiches, and ravioli platters. "Hungry brides don't exist in the Copperfield family." She dropped onto the couch between Julia and Ella and wrapped her wrinkled hand around Julia's as Aunt Alana hurried to join them. Anna made sure to take a photograph of them all together—three Copperfield girls in their forties and their mother, the proudest Copperfield of all.

Anna was lucky enough to ride with her mother up to the venue, where she met with Violet to take over Adam's responsibilities. Violet was already in "wedding planner mode," with a microscopic microphone extending to her mouth. No curl on her head was out of place, and she wore the perfect lavender dress—one that bore a resemblance to Jennifer Lopez's when she played a fictional wedding planner.

Violet seemed to float with importance. Just as soon as Adam was back in Anna's arms, Violet clacked off, speaking into her microphone.

"She already has four weddings lined up for this autumn," Julia muttered as they headed toward the back of the venue to get ready. "The woman is fantastic at marketing herself. I should take a page out of her book for the publishing house." Julia smiled and took Adam's foot in her hand. "This suit is really something, isn't it? He looks like a mini James Bond."

Anna laughed and checked in his diaper bag to find the shoes, which they immediately tried on him when they reached the back room. Adam kicked and squabbled, not accustomed to having thick, heavy things on his feet.

"I understand, little guy," Julia joked, showing off her stilettos, which she'd chosen for the ceremony. "Fashion is pain."

"He can get away with anything," Scarlet said. "It's not fair."

As a favor to his mother and grandmother, Adam slept peacefully in his carrier over the next few hours. Hairstylists and makeup technicians arrived to beautify the Copperfield women, bringing with them a wave of gossip. They learned about a jilted bride from last weekend, a mother-of-the-groom who'd hated the bride so much that she'd refused to sit for the ceremony, a flower girl who'd gotten a nosebleed midway down the aisle.

"What about you?" one of the makeup technicians demanded. "Any drama here?"

Julia sputtered with laughter. "He's my high school sweetheart. We both married other people, and we're coming back together again."

"That isn't drama," the technician said. "That's just romantic."

When it was time, Anna helped her mother into her dress and buttoned it to the top. She remembered how

A Winter's Miracle

she'd called it quasi-Stevie Nicks to Smith, who'd adored the description. Now, she saw she'd been wrong. The dress was precisely Julia's style—no one else's. Julia's eyes glowed as she extended her hand for Anna to take.

"I wouldn't have been strong enough to get here without you," she said softly.

Anna wasn't sure that was true. Her mother had always done exactly what she wanted. That power had always been within her.

"Thank you for showing me what love is all about," Anna breathed.

The Copperfield women walked slowly to the entranceway outside the wedding venue. Bernard awaited them with tears in his eyes, his hands clasped over his waist. He was dressed in a brand-new tuxedo, as the one he'd left behind before prison no longer fit. Apparently, Bernard and Greta had had a blissful afternoon of shopping in Boston, trying on gowns and tuxedos, getting tipsy at wineries.

It was impossible to imagine what it was like to have loved someone that long. Anna hoped, one day, she'd understand.

Just before the ceremony was set to begin, Adam kicked and screeched in his carrier, and Anna picked him up again. He blinked around at them, mystified by their beautiful gowns and their red lipstick.

"It looks like he wants to go down the aisle with you," Julia said.

Anna laughed. "He loves to be a part of it all."

Julia had selected four bridesmaids—her sisters, Alana and Ella, and her daughters, Rachel and Anna. Anna went last, carrying her bouquet in one hand and Adam in her other arm. As she walked, her heels dug into the rug, and she teetered, laughing at herself. As everyone gasped and giggled at Adam's surprise appearance in the aisle, she scoured their faces, searching for Smith. He was nowhere to be found.

Both Bernard and Greta walked Julia down the aisle. This was only the second wedding they'd been able to attend for one of their children, and their tears were constant. When they passed Julia off to Charlie, Greta and Bernard held one another in the front row, gazing up at Julia. They had no eyes for Charlie.

Anna allowed herself a moment's fantasy of her own future wedding. She wasn't sure she'd ask her father to walk her down the aisle, though. She could only imagine her mother in that role.

Adam was respectful during the ceremony, which earned him the title of "best-behaved baby at a wedding." Anna laughed as she carried him through the venue, back toward the reception hall, waving at onlookers. Adam was a celebrity.

Violet had decorated the reception hall impeccably, with floral arrangements glowing beneath chandeliers, gorgeous place settings, and a five-piece string orchestra that played Beethoven as the guests ambled through with their first glasses of champagne. As Violet whipped here and there, Anna managed to nab her for a moment and compliment her. "It's something special," she said.

Violet's grin was ear to ear. "You know, I keep asking myself if I still believe in love after everything that happened. And I think my answer to myself is here, in everything I did for this ceremony. It's proof of something. Don't you think?"

Just then, someone in her earpiece howled with a problem, and Violet scampered off, begging whoever was on the other line to keep calm. Anna smiled to herself and squeezed Adam's hand. It was nearly time for him to nap again.

The wedding feast was nearly as good as Greta's cooking. Only nearly. All of the Copperfield family members made sure to mention this as they ate, their eyes on Greta — "If only you'd been the cook. But we're glad you can sit with us. We're glad you can celebrate instead." Of the turkey, Bernard said, "It's slightly dry, isn't it?" Greta only smiled in response. Anna laughed to herself. It was amazing what we did for the people we loved—falling all over ourselves to build them up.

Just before Charlie and Julia's first dance, Bernard stood to make a toast. He raised his glass to the happy married couple and spoke beautifully about the first time he'd met Charlie. "I always knew you two were carved from the same cloth. It's been a weaving, winding road to get us here today. But I'm over the moon to celebrate your love."

Anna imagined her grandfather locked away in a prison cell, learning of his children's weddings—Julia's, Alana's, and Quentin's. He was stronger than anyone she knew, coming back from that.

Anna's eyes flitted through the reception hall as Julia and Charlie swayed in time to the music. Adam was asleep in the next room, and she clutched the baby monitor like her life depended on it.

When she spotted him, her heart jumped into her throat. She would have recognized those blue eyes anywhere. She would have spotted him in any crowd.

As the DJ gathered the other lovers to the dance floor to join Charlie and Julia, Anna pierced through the crowd, drawn toward him like a magnet. Smith hovered at the edge of everyone else, his hands shoved in his pants pockets, his wild hair tamed with gel. His smile looked sadder, and his eyes were rimmed with red. It was only when Anna got closer to him that she realized he was crying.

"Smith!" she whispered.

Smith took her chin in his hand and gazed into her eyes. Anna felt all of their emails to one another—a brimming collection of longing. She felt expectation. And before she could stop herself, she raised onto her toes and kissed him with her eyes closed. The world of life and music and color swirled around her, but she remained in Smith's warm embrace. It was the sort of kiss you changed your life over. It was cinematic.

When their kiss broke, Anna swallowed him with a hug and painted his suit with tears. "When did you get here?" she asked. "Are you all right?"

Before Smith could answer, Violet breezed past and smiled adoringly at Smith. She patted his shoulder and said, "You look wonderful."

"It was a perfect recommendation. Thank you." Smith's smile was crooked.

"Welcome back, Smith," Violet said. "It'll be good to have you on the island again. I haven't known who to cook for!"

Anna's heart swelled. She glanced from Smith to Violet and back again. They'd surprised her.

Before Anna could think of anything to say, the baby monitor vibrated in her hand, and Adam's cries echoed between them. He always needed her. It gave her gravity in an otherwise aimless world.

"Uh-oh," Violet said. "I'd go, but I have about a million problems in the kitchen. You wouldn't believe the stress of a wedding planner." Even as she said it, her eyes gleamed with happiness. Maybe this was her new gravity.

Smith laced his fingers through Anna's as she guided him to the quiet room to the left of the venue, where the last of the blue light of the day spilled across the carpet directly beside Adam's carrier. Adam kicked his legs happily, and his fingers fluttered just beyond his taut sleeves. With a flourish, Anna picked him up and bobbed him around as he giggled. His eyes danced to Smith's.

"He remembers you," Anna said, although she wasn't sure that was true. How long were babies' memories?

"Even if he doesn't," Smith said, "I'm not going anywhere ever again." He took Adam in his arms and danced across the carpet, wiggling Adam's hand. When he glanced back up, his eyes were illuminated. And he said, "My brother, Freddie, will be here tomorrow."

Anna's heart opened. In Smith's eyes, she recognized a future—one of hardships, promises, and responsibilities.

In some ways, she would become Freddie's "mother." And that would be an entirely different proposition altogether.

"I can't wait," Anna whispered. She cleared the distance between herself and Smith to wrap her arms around them. She prayed for the strength to lift all of her loved ones up—to carry them through the hardships of life, to have the strength that all mothers were allowed. She prayed, forever, for the power to go on.

Coming Next in the Nantucket Sunset Series
Pre Order Nantucket Solstice

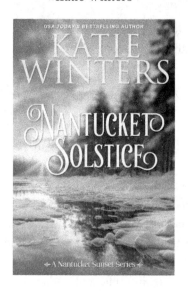

Other Books by Katie

The Vineyard Sunset Series
A Nantucket Sunset Series
Secrets of Mackinac Island Series
Sisters of Edgartown Series
A Katama Bay Series
A Mount Desert Island Series
The Coleman Series

Printed in the USA
CPSIA information can be obtained
at www.ICGtesting.com
CBHW050526270724
12290CB00010B/386